I0659935

Lawyers
Never
Lie
a novel

Lawyers
Never
Lie

a novel

T E R I
KANEFIELD

Cover design by Streetlight Graphics

www.terikanefield.com

ISBN-13: 978-0692283547

For Andy

1

Eric came into the kitchen whistling the theme song from the Jetsons. I looked up, startled. It had been weeks since Eric had been in a cheerful mood.

"What's going on?" I asked.

"Guess who just called."

"Tom?"

Tom was the general contractor who had recently trashed our house and disappeared.

"Guess again," said Eric.

"Tom's wife?"

"Nope. Tom's lawyer."

"Tom's got a lawyer? Good. Now maybe things will start making sense."

Good. Now maybe things will start making sense isn't what most people say when a lawyer calls, particularly the lawyer representing the contractor who just trashed their house. But I'd just recently graduated from law school. If you've ever been called for jury duty and watched that video the courts show about how jurors are doing a patriotic and civic duty, with the flags waving and America the Beautiful playing in the background and everyone smiling as justice is dispensed, you'll understand how I felt coming out of law school.

When I quit my teaching job to go to law school, my students gave me adoring cards, which I taped around the arched entryway to our dining room. One of our neighbors, a lawyer, read some of the cards and warned me that if I enjoyed being adored, I should not go to law school. I responded with the good lawyers could do. Wasn't history filled with lawyers who had been engineers of social change? Just look at Thurgood Marshall and Charles Hamilton Houston. He asked, "Why do you think there are all those lawyer jokes?" Being naive, I answered, "Because people are jealous?"

I figured talking to Tom's lawyer had to be better than trying to talk to Tom. Talking to Tom had been a lot like trying to talk to a cinderblock.

"I'll call him tomorrow," I told Eric.

"Not *him*," he said, handing me a post-it note with a name and phone number. "*Her*."

It took a moment to decipher Eric's scrawl. "Does this say *Paula Armstrong*? Oh my God! I know Paula. Or I did, a long time ago. She lived in my college dorm! I had some classes with her!"

"Good," Eric said. "Tell her that her client owes us money."

"If this is the same Paula Armstrong I knew, telling her might not do much good. She was a bit of a bulldozer."

"If Tom hired a lawyer, he must know he's in trouble."

That was in January, when Eric was still optimistic.

The next day I stopped by the house to pick up a few things. We'd moved into a nearby apartment because our house resembled a disaster area. In our bedroom, cold air was coming in through the holes in the floor of the closet. A blue plastic tarp covered the opening to the new closet where there was supposed to be a door, but no door could be hung because the doorframe was crooked. Sawdust covered the dresser mirror and the framed drawings Jocelyn had done in third grade.

My cell phone rang.

"Hello," I said.

"Is this Cassie Sanders?" The woman's voice was clipped and businesslike.

"Yes." My last name wasn't Sanders. It was Eisen. I didn't change my name when I married Eric, but I never corrected anyone who called me Cassie Sanders.

"This is Paula Armstrong. I represent Tom Mullin. I would like for us to clear up this misunderstanding as soon as possible." Her tone was formal and commanding with a la-dee-da quality. Paula obviously hadn't figured out that I was really Cassie Eisen—or if she had, she didn't care.

I felt disoriented. Breastfeeding left me tired, and Rebecca had kept me up most of the night.

"I'm glad you called," I said. "We've got a real mess here."

"*Do* you now?" The way she emphasized "do" made her sound sarcastic instead of polite. "Tom's position is that he wants to finish the project, so I need to know when he can come back on the property."

"I don't think you understand. We didn't hear from him for weeks so we hired other people to finish the work. He left us without water. We have a newborn baby. We had no telephone service for ten days because his workers left the wires draped on the ground and trampled on them. And he blew up the kitchen light."

She didn't say anything, so I repeated. "He blew up the kitchen light. He was working in the back of the house, as far from the kitchen as you can get."

I had been home with the kids when all the lights brightened, followed by a bang from the kitchen and the smell of smoke. Afraid the house was about to catch fire, I'd gathered the kids in Nathan's room because of the quick exit through the small bathroom to the backyard. That was late November, so I already suspected that Tom was a walking safety hazard. An electrician later explained that Tom had thrown the wrong voltage through the house.

"Did you ever give him a chance to fix the light?" she asked.

The baby, Rebecca, started fussing.

"Have you ever had a baby?" I asked.

"As a matter of fact, I have—" Whatever she said next was drowned out by the baby's wail.

I paced with Rebecca to quiet her. "Then maybe you can understand what it has been like, with a newborn and a house torn apart."

"Did you ever give him a chance to fix the kitchen light?"

"He had five weeks to fix it, but he never did. How could he? All his employees quit. Then he brought in those temporary people. One was an out-of-work travel agent with no building experience whatsoever—"

"Then you understand that it wasn't his fault," she said.

"Whose fault was it? The Easter Bunny's? Tom was the general contractor. He was responsible."

"Did Tom blow up the kitchen light?" she asked. "Or was it one of his crew?"

"It was Tom. There was no crew that week."

This conversation was going nowhere. It felt like talking to Tom all over again. Something moved behind the blue tarp. For a moment I thought Tom was in the house. We had no way of securing the house. Anyone willing to crawl on his belly could get in. But it was just the cat pushing her way into the bedroom and rubbing against my leg, her fur cold from the outdoors.

Paula said, "I need to know when Tom can come back to finish the project—"

The baby wailed louder.

I disconnected the phone and immediately called Eliza, my best friend of twenty years. Eliza taught art history in Oakland. I knew from her tone that she didn't have much time to chat.

"You'll never guess who our contractor hired to represent him," I said.

"Someone famous?"

"No. Someone we know. Well, someone we used to know."

Silence. More silence. "I give up," she said.

"Here's a hint. The secretary in charge of Reynolds Residence Hall."

"Paula Armstrong? You're kidding! What did she say?"

"I don't think she knew it was me. If she ever gets around to reading the contract, she'll figure it out."

"Did she try to defend the guy?"

"Oh, yes. And she tried to bully me."

"That's Paula. I'm not surprised." And then, "I have a meeting. Email me the whole story."

"I will. Bye."

Eric always said he wanted ten children, but he'd settle for five. After our twins Nathan and Jocelyn were born, he said, well, maybe, two or three children would be ideal. As it turned out, the twins so absorbed our time that we didn't even think about more children until the twins were nine. Suddenly they seemed more independent—less eager to go to the zoo, no longer clamoring for rides on Eric's back, going into their own bedrooms for hours at a time to play. I missed the weight of a baby on my shoulder and Eric remembered he wanted lots of kids, so we tried again.

Well, nothing. After one year, we went to a fertility specialist who said we both tested very fertile. She said that despite our ages—I was thirty-six and Eric was forty—the tests showed that we'd probably conceive within a year.

Another year passed, and then another. We accepted that it just wasn't going to happen. I was tired of teaching, so I figured I'd settle for a new career.

One morning during my third year of law school I got out of bed, and the room spun around dizzily. I leaned against the wall until I could get into the bathroom, where I threw up. Later that morning, thinking it couldn't be true, I bought a drugstore pregnancy test. I didn't believe the bright purple line on the test strip until I threw up again the following morning. So when people assume that the baby was a surprise and that a thirteen-year gap between the children was not planned, they're not completely wrong.

In our temporary apartment, we slept in sleeping bags on air mattresses. Boxes and piles of stuff were everywhere. The baby never slept more than three hours at a stretch, so I was perpetually exhausted. Neither Eric nor I had had a chance to organize anything. We ate dinner at a scuffed wooden kitchen table on paper plates. The twins said living in our apartment was like camping.

That evening we were eating pizza and salad. Nathan said, "Mom, I have a legal question. Can you get in trouble for breaking a rule if the rule isn't written down somewhere?"

Eric put down his fork and looked at Nathan. "Don't do it, Nathan."

"Oh, Eric," I said. "Why do you have to assume the worst? He's asking a hypothetical question."

Jocelyn gave her newly acquired teen-aged smirk. "Mom,

he's thinking about breaking a rule that's not written down. Or he wouldn't ask that."

"Will everyone stop this cynical stuff, and let Nathan talk?" I turned to Nathan. "Okay, sweetie. What do you mean, if it isn't written somewhere?"

I hoped he was learning about the constitutional ban on *ex post facto* laws in school. What he said was: "If it isn't in the school manual or list of rules, can you get in trouble for it?"

I wasn't naive enough to tell a thirteen-year-old he couldn't get in trouble for doing something not specifically against the rules. "Yes," I said. "You can get in trouble. Some rules are so general they apply to lots of things. For example, you're not allowed to do something risky that will endanger yourself or anyone else."

"But if it's something that isn't dangerous," said Nathan.

Eric said, "Give us an example, Nathan."

"I don't have an example." Nathan reached across the table for more pizza.

"Don't reach," I said, and to demonstrate good manners: "Will someone please pass Nathan the pizza?" But it was too late. Nathan had already seized a piece from the tray.

"Sorry," Nathan said, dripping cheese across the table.

"Give us an example, Nathan," said Eric again. "What rule can be broken that isn't written in the manual?"

"Like, for example, getting up on the roof of the school," said Nathan.

Eric looked steadily at Nathan and said, "Don't do it."

"He's not going to," I said. "Nathan, are you planning to get on the school roof?"

"No." His voice took on the highly-pitched squeak that meant he was becoming annoyed. "I just want to know if you do something that's not in the rules, can you get in trouble?"

"Yes," I said. "You can."

"But," said Nathan, "you'd have an argument in your defense if it wasn't in the rules."

"So what?" I said. "Your argument would be weak and you'd be in trouble."

"But I'd have an argument," Nathan insisted.

Jocelyn said, "He's going to get up on the roof, Mom. I know him."

"No, he's not," I said. "Nathan wouldn't do that." To make sure, I asked once more, "You're not planning to get on the roof, are you, Nathan?"

Nathan gave a grunt that sounded like "No," and then reached across the table for more pizza. Eric stopped him from reaching and I demonstrated again: "Will someone please pass Nathan the pizza?"

The next day, I drove over to the house to check on the workers. We'd recently hired a carpenter and handyman. In front of our house was a white pickup truck with the city of Sacramento logo. A stocky man wearing jeans and carrying a clipboard was taping a yellow piece of paper to the door. I parked behind the truck and unstrapped the baby from the car seat and put her in her cloth carrier.

The man approached me and held out his hand for me to shake. He was tanned with a beard and hair that fell unevenly over his ears. He walked with an air of authority. "I'm Bill, a city inspector," he said, extending his hand. "Are you the homeowner?"

"Yes, I am."

To make sure, he pointed to our house and said, "This is your house? Tom Mullin is your contractor?"

"This is my house. He *was* our contractor."

"I had a feeling he wasn't on the job anymore. I was hoping to be able to talk to you in person. I didn't want to give you the bad news over the phone."

He watched me as if waiting for permission to give me the bad news.

"Go ahead," I said.

"Your contractor was given five correction notices since August. He was supposed to make the corrections before moving on to the next stage of the construction. Looks to me like he just kept on building."

Bill took a manila folder from his clipboard, and from the folder he took five yellow cards with orange borders. "Have you ever seen any of these?"

"No," I said, looking at the cards. They were five-by-seven-inch cards with handwritten notes that at first appeared illegible. Then I saw that the words were some kind of builder's jargon with reference to code numbers.

Bill said, "I specifically told him not to put up the sheetrock until he made the corrections and his work could be inspected."

I needed to sit down. The birth had gone well, but it had been only seven weeks, so I tired easily. I leaned back against the car.

"Let me see if I understand this," I said. "You came and inspected and saw problems with his work. You gave him correction notices and told him that he couldn't continue building until he made the corrections. He didn't make the corrections, and he kept building."

"It looks that way."

From where we stood, you couldn't even see that the house was under construction. The addition was for a simple room added to the end of the hallway. Part of the addition was a walk-in closet for the master bedroom. The other part was a small room for the baby. The only complication was that the electrical panel, main water valve, and gas meter had to be moved. Everyone told us it was a simple, straightforward job. In fact, the first contractor we met didn't want the job because it was too small for him. He looked at the plans and said, "Anyone can do this." As it turned out, he was wrong.

"What are we supposed to do now?" I said.

"That's where the bad news comes in."

"That wasn't the bad news?"

"The bad news," he said, "is that we're going to have to open the walls and inspect. Here's the number for you to call to set up an appointment." He handed me a card.

"Thanks." I was exhausted and felt a crying jag coming on.

He waved and got into his truck. I stood watching him drive away, then went to the front porch to gather the mail that was too large to fit through the slot. The paper the city inspector had taped to the door was a handwritten note asking us to call and arrange a time for an inspector to visit. I went inside and sat on the couch. The baby was still sleeping. I put my head back and closed my eyes.

My way of dealing with stress was to go to sleep, a quirk Eric didn't discover until the second year of our marriage when my wedding ring slipped off and washed down the kitchen drain. Eric, being a practical person of action, immediately fetched his tools and took the sink apart. The task took him a half hour. He found the ring caught on a drain trap just under the sink. "Hey Cassie," he called out. No answer. He found me lying across the bed, asleep. He shook me gently. "Cassie?" I opened my eyes, remembered the ring, groaned, and closed my eyes again. "I got the ring!" he said. "Look!" I distinctly remember the feeling of relief that flooded through me.

Looking back, it occurred to me that Eric had fulfilled my

deepest wish: When confronted with a problem, I would go to sleep, wake up, and the problem would be gone.

I was awakened by the vibrating of my cell phone. Thinking it was Eric, I opened my cell phone without checking to see who was calling. "Hello?"

"Mrs. Sanders?" I didn't recognize the man's voice.

"Yes?" I said.

"Good morning. I'm Vice Principal Reynolds, calling from McIntosh Middle School. I have your son Nathan here in the office."

"Why?" I said. If I hadn't been so tired and off balance, I would have known exactly why.

"Nathan climbed up on the school roof."

I groaned.

"We're only suspending him for one day. It could have been worse. At first, he was cheeky with us, but then he settled down and just apologized."

I knew what he had done that was cheeky: He had given his *ex post facto* argument about how he couldn't be punished for breaking a rule that wasn't written anywhere.

"I'll be right over to get him," I said.

2

When you have twins, you're not supposed to compare them, but when your twins are as different as ours, you really can't help it. Nathan had Eric's dark hair; Jocelyn's was honey-brown. Nathan had pale skin with bluish undertones and blue eyes. Jocelyn's skin was darker, and her eyes were brown. Nathan was a social butterfly who cared more about play than work; Jocelyn took school seriously. Nathan was mischievous; Jocelyn was the model child.

We were having breakfast on a Sunday morning during my second year of law school when I explained my career choice to the kids. I told them what criminal defense attorneys do, and what appellate attorneys do, and what it meant that I would file appeals for people who'd been convicted of crimes. I also explained that I would take only court-appointed cases—clients who could not afford to hire a lawyer.

I could tell from the way they paid close attention, then sat quietly, that they had questions. Finally Jocelyn said, "Lawyers aren't supposed to lie, right?"

"Right," I said.

"But if lawyers aren't supposed to lie," Jocelyn asked, "how can you represent someone who is guilty?"

It was like Jocelyn to come up with a question like that. I

went for the simplest possible explanation: "Remember about how you feel when Dad is really mad at you for something?"

Eric was the disciplinarian. I was the soft touch.

"Okay," she said, waiting for me to continue.

"When Dad is really mad at you for something, do you ever wish someone was completely on your side? Do you wish you could explain why what you did really wasn't as bad as it looked? Do you wish you could remind him that you're a great kid, even though you did something he didn't like? Do you ever think your punishment was unfair?"

This seemed to satisfy her.

It was Nathan who was not satisfied. He said, "But if they're guilty."

"Sometimes when Dad is mad at you, you're guilty. But aren't you still a great kid? Don't you wish Dad would just understand why you did it?"

"But if they're guilty," he said again. He crossed his arms over his chest, and I knew he wasn't going to budge.

Nathan was sitting in the vice principal's office waiting for me.

"I need a lawyer," he said.

"This isn't funny, Nathan." I signed the forms to get him released from school. We were driving back to the apartment when I said, "Do you know what happened last night when we went for a walk?" After dinner we'd all gone for a walk— except Nathan, who had stayed home to play computer games.

"What?" he said.

"Cocoa was following us." Cocoa was Jocelyn's cat, her eleventh-year birthday present, a black cat with a white spot on her tail we'd gotten from the animal shelter. I said, "Cocoa ran into the street, right in front of a car. The driver hit the brakes. There was an awful screech, but the car missed Cocoa."

Ordinarily Nathan would have rolled his eyes and said, *Get on with it, Mom. What's the point?* But when Nathan wasn't sure how much trouble he was in, he tended to be more polite.

"Do you know what Jocelyn said to Cocoa?" I asked.

Nathan shook his head. How would he know?

"She said, 'Cocoa, if you're going to die, please don't die because you did something totally stupid.'"

He waited. I didn't explain. Eventually he understood. "Getting on the roof wasn't totally stupid," he said.

"It was dumber than stupid. And you lied. You told me you weren't going to do it."

"I wasn't," Nathan said.

"Nathan. You said you wouldn't, and you did. So you lied."

"No," he said in an exaggeratedly patient tone. "I told you I wasn't *planning* to do it. And I wasn't *planning* to do it then. I didn't *plan* to do it until later."

When the twins were twelve, a family friend asked them if they planned to go to law school. Jocelyn said, "Yes, I'm going to Berkeley like Mom." Nathan, who had mostly been struck by how much work was required of law students but was nonetheless interested in a high salary, said, "No, I'm going to marry a lawyer."

Sometimes, though, I honestly thought Nathan would be the lawyer—not, please understand, because of his disregard for rules and apparent lying, but because of his willingness to try absurd arguments and his ability to distinguish between planning to get on the roof and simply bringing the subject up for discussion.

At home, I sent Nathan to his room. I probably should have gotten angrier and come up with a harsher punishment. Eric always said I was too soft on the kids.

You'd think, being the softie in the family that I'd been the one to hire Tom. In fact, Eric made the decision because I was I afraid I'd hire a bad contractor, which is funny when you think about it.

Eric, who regularly hired and fired people as part of his job as product manager for a lawn and garden products company, took the task of hiring a contractor seriously. After he talked to the contractor who did a lot of work in our neighborhood, the one who disdainfully told Eric the job was too small for him, Eric got the idea to ask Mark, our draftsperson, for recommendations. Mark gave Eric four names. Eric interviewed each of the four. One would not be able to start for a year. Another never gave a written bid. He looked at the house and plans, thought for a minute and said, "I can only give an approximate price. I won't know for sure what's involved until I get in there."

That seemed way too risky, so we were down to two.

Both Tom and the other guy said they could start within a month. Both Tom and the other guy said the project could not possibly take longer than four months. But only Tom was willing to put his promises in writing and into the contract.

The other contractor furnished two references. Both his references reported that his workmanship was good, but he always ran behind schedule. When Eric asked Tom for the names of references, Tom said, "I can show you my work." He said he was finishing a project just a few miles away. His crew was still working at the house.

The next morning, Eric met Tom over at the house. The homeowners were not there, but Tom's crew was putting on the finishing touches, working from a "punch list" the owner had drawn up of the final things that needed to be done before making the final payment.

Tom showed Eric around and let Eric inspect the bathroom he had remodeled and the family room he added. The crew was polite and answered Eric's questions. Eric reported that Tom's workmanship was excellent. Except for a change in style—the added family room was airier and more open than the original house—you could not tell where the original house ended and the addition began.

Eric, impressed that Tom had been willing to show his work-in-progress, checked Tom's license with the license board and called the Better Business Bureau to see if there were any complaints against him. His license checked out and there were no complaints against him. We signed the contract with Tom Mullin in late May, six months before the baby was due.

Signing a contract is like saying "I do" at the altar: At the moment of signing, you're not imagining that the promises might fall apart.

Eric came home early that evening because it was second-semester back-to-school night. When Eric learned what had happened, he told Nathan he was grounded for a week. The issue was whether Nathan would be allowed to attend the back-to-school night. Ordinarily Nathan had no interest in attending back-to-school nights, but now he wanted to go. I knew he was tired of sitting in his room with nothing to do.

"You're grounded," Eric reminded him.

"I have a right to be present when my teachers might be talking about me," he said.

It wasn't even worth arguing that he had no such right. Eric and I looked at each other. I gave a little shrug. Eric said, "Fine, Nathan, you can go."

He whooped and said, "Today is my lucky day—Tuesday, January thirteenth."

"If you call getting suspended from school lucky," Jocelyn said. "Besides, the *un*lucky day is *Friday* the Thirteenth."

"Not in South America," Nathan told her. "In South America, the *lucky* day is *Tuesday* the Thirteenth."

Jocelyn looked at me and said, "He makes up facts."

"Don't pay attention," I advised.

After arriving at the school, we split into two groups: Eric and Nathan went to visit Nathan's classrooms, Jocelyn and I went to hers. I carried Rebecca, asleep in a baby sling.

Jocelyn's history teacher, Mr. Kent, complained to the parents about how he had not been able to get the funding he expected from the district to take the students to a particular play in San Francisco. Suddenly, he stopped.

"Do any of you work for the government?" he asked. I understood why he was asking. A lot of people in Sacramento held state government jobs.

Jocelyn's hand went up. When she had the teacher's attention, she said proudly: "My mother works *against* the government."

Mr. Kent blinked and drew back, surprised. His hair was long, and you had the feeling he didn't so much mind people who worked against the government, but he was uncomfortable, so I explained: "I studied to be a criminal defense lawyer." It felt strange to say that. I had been a lawyer for exactly six weeks.

He gave his head a shake as if to say, all right, let's move on.

Before Jocelyn and I left, Mr. Kent shook my hand and said, "I have Nathan in sixth-period English. I should have guessed that one of his parents was a lawyer."

"Oh, no. What did he do this time?"

"I had the class sign an agreement outlining the students' responsibilities, and mine. After class Nathan informed me that minors can't be held to contracts."

While studying for the bar exam, I'd used a set of prepared flashcards with cartoon characters and hypothetical situations to make legal points. Nathan found the cards hilarious, particularly the Donald Duck contracts cards. He took to reading the cards for fun and consequently picked up some understanding of contract law.

"What did you say?" I asked.

"I said, 'Well then, don't act like a minor.'"

It was a good answer, but I suspected Nathan would act like a minor for a long time to come.

3

Eric met me at the house the following day during his lunch time so we could talk to the city inspectors. Nathan, suspended from school, was with us. We also asked Big Dan, our new handyman, to come as well. It was easy enough to see how Big Dan got his nickname. His head came close to the top of the doorframe. Big Dan brought his sheetrock-cutting tools.

"What's all this?" asked Clifford, one of the city inspectors, pointing to the places where the sheetrock had been cut and patched. The other inspector, Bill, was checking notes on a clipboard.

Eric said, "Tom put up the sheetrock before he finished running all the wires, so he had to keep cutting and patching the sheetrock."

That was exactly the kind of thing that drove Eric crazy. Eric was a master of efficiency, which was why he was so good at his job. He spent his days figuring out ways for production to run more smoothly. So naturally it drove him crazy that Tom kept cutting the sheetrock to run the electrical wires. Each week Tom's sheetrock guy came in to patch the sheetrock that Tom had cut. After a month or so, the walls looked like a patched quilt, or the roadmap to Crazytown. I said it was like Penelope. Eric asked who Penelope was. I said, "You know, Penelope in the myth, who spent her days weaving, and then spent her nights unweaving what she had done that day." Eric didn't answer. When I said things like that, he usually didn't answer.

Clifford pointed to a place on the wall, and Big Dan took out his tools and cut a hole. "Would you look at that!" Big Dan boomed.

The inspectors bent to look. "Oh Lordy," said Clifford.

I went to look. A bolt about a half-inch was shaped like an "S."

"What's wrong with it?" I asked.

"It's supposed to be straight," Big Dan said. "Bent like that, it's not structural anymore. I could break that bolt right over my knee."

Clifford explained: "That steel piece is screwed to the frame. The bolt is embedded in the concrete slab. The whole thing anchors the frame to the foundation."

Big Dan added, "So if we get a good strong wind, the room will stay put. That's why it's called a hold-down."

I had a vision of a strong wind snapping the bolts and lifting the room into the clouds, like Dorothy's farmhouse, with my baby inside.

Big Dan lifted away part of the plywood floor to reveal a metal box. Clifford opened the box. Inside was a spectacular tangle of wires. Some of the heavier black ones were badly frayed. The mess of wires continued up through the wall.

"That's why he put up the sheetrock before running all the wires," Eric said. "He wanted to cover up this mess. That son of a bitch."

Clifford said, "You need to get an electrician in here as soon as possible. You have some serious fire hazards."

Bill looked at the tangle of wires and said, "Nobody in his right mind would do this." He looked up and asked, "Did you ever see signs that your contractor was using drugs?"

The question took me by surprise. I looked at Eric. "Well," I said. "Maybe."

"Could be," Eric agreed. "He was always falling asleep in the backyard. When the kids tried to wake him up, he wouldn't budge."

"And he was always getting sick," I said, "either the flu, or a cold, or something. He had a lot of backaches and spent a lot of time with a chiropractor. For a robust-looking fellow, his health was pretty bad."

"And his dog died a few times," Nathan said.

"Excuse me?" said Clifford. He'd been writing on his clipboard. Now he turned to look at Nathan.

"Well," I said, "obviously he forgot he'd already used that excuse."

Eric said, "Cassie thought maybe he had more than one dog named Buddy. It takes her a while to believe someone might be a bad person. But I knew by then he was a lying sack."

"And sometimes," I said, "we'd have conversations with him, and then a few days later, he wouldn't remember anything about the conversation."

"He remembered," said Eric. "He's a lying sack."

Clifford said, "You know, you could probably file a charge with the district attorney for criminal negligence. Looks like he deliberately concealed these errors."

Eric said, "My wife is a lawyer."

The two inspectors and Big Dan looked at me. Once, when I was in law school, one of my college roommates, who had been practicing law for fifteen years, said that whereas a lot of people don't like lawyers, they do like law students. "Sort of the way a tiger cub is still cute and harmless," was her explanation.

"I'm a very new lawyer, so I hardly count."

Clifford and Bill wrote down all the things that remained to be done on yellow correction notices. In addition to hold-downs and wiring that needed to be done, there were roof tiles missing, the final coat of stucco had not been applied, the doors had not been hung, the door to the attic was not installed properly, and the trim and the baseboard had not been installed.

"Call if you have any questions," Clifford said.

"Would you be willing to testify for us, if we need it?" I asked.

"Certianly," said Clifford. "There is a request form to fill out at the office, and a small fee that goes to the city."

After the inspectors left, Big Dan said, "You got to get your plans and permit back. That Tom guy wasn't supposed to take them from the property. I learned that in my contractor's class."

"We've left messages demanding them back," I said.

"Give me his number," said Big Dan. "I'll get them back for you."

His utter confidence—and his three-hundred-pound hulking body—worried me. "What are you going to do?"

My tone must have given away my fears because he laughed. "I'm not going to say anything wrong. I promise. You can listen to everything I say."

Eric shrugged and gave him Tom's phone number. Big Dan punched the numbers into his cell phone and called Tom. He introduced himself as Big Dan. He explained who he was. He said he was at our house. He said we needed the permit and plans back immediately, and offered to go get the plans and permit, wherever they might be.

There was nothing wrong in what he said. It was the depth of his voice, the fact that his tone never wavered, or perhaps his name "Big Dan" or some combination, along with a threat so veiled that you couldn't point to it. The conversation lasted less than two minutes.

Big Dan came back into the room and said, "Someone'll be here shortly to bring the plans and permit. I'll wait outside."

"For Tom," Eric said, "shortly can mean anything up to and including two weeks."

"It won't be that long," said Big Dan. "I'll call him back if I have to. I always finish what I start." He laughed. "And don't worry. I won't do anything wrong."

While we waited, Eric made a batch of the twins' favorite cinnamon muffins. I needed a nap. I slept on Jocelyn's bed. I woke up about a half hour later to the smell of warm cinnamon muffins.

When I came into the room, Big Dan was seated at the dining room table picking crumbs off a plate. "Those muffins are great!" he said. "I need the recipe."

"They're healthy, too," I told him. "Eric makes them with applesauce instead of oil and almost no sugar."

"Aww!" Big Dan said. "Don't tell me that! But they're as good as regular."

A car pulled up in front of the house. Big Dan looked out of the dining room window and said, "I'll bet that's him." He went outside. Eric and I watched through the shutters. Someone in the car handed Big Dan a scroll of papers. As the car pulled away, Big Dan waved. Then he came back into the house, triumphant. "Here they are," he said. "Your plans and the permit. I told you I finish what I start."

"Amazing," I said. "Who brought them over?"

"Some girl named Kristin." Kristin was the former travel agent who had been working as Tom's assistant during his last week on the job. I was surprised she was still working for him. Few of his employees lasted as long as three weeks.

Eric wrote a check for Big Dan's time, including the time he spent waiting for the return of the plans and permit. Big Dan folded the check and put it into his shirt pocket without reading it.

"Looks to me," said Big Dan, "like when all is said and done, that guy is going to owe you for a lot of repairs. If you have any trouble collecting from him, you let me know. I can get him to pay up."

"We appreciate that," I said, "but I don't think we'll have trouble collecting." What I meant was that we're fairly conventional people and just wouldn't feel right hiring a handyman-collection-agency.

"Oh, yeah, I forgot," Big Dan said, laughing. "You're a lawyer. That's even scarier than me!"

I pointed out that a lawyer obviously wasn't scarier because I hadn't been able to get the plans and permit back.

He laughed again. "Also looks to me like you're going to have a lot of handyman work to do around here. I'm as good at rebuilding doorframes and putting up sheetrock as I am at getting back plans and permits. And I'll testify for you, no charge."

4

From the window over the kitchen sink in the apartment, I could see across the parking lot to the driveway. This meant I could watch for Eric from the kitchen. You could set your watch by Eric's habits. He left his office by 5:30 and drove to the house, a drive that took him about a half hour. He picked up our mail and checked on the construction, and arrived at the apartment in plenty of time for dinner at 6:30. It was now close to 7:00. The enchiladas were warming in the oven, the salad was on the table, and Eric was nowhere in sight. I'd called him, but his cell phone was turned off.

The apartment smelled of pine and cedar. That was because when we first moved in, the apartment—while perfectly clean—had the moldy smell of an old attic. I aired the rooms, cleaned once more, and put cedar chips and pine shavings in the closets and under the kitchen sink. The place still didn't smell like home, but the musty smell was gone.

As if sensing that I was worried and needed a distraction, Jocelyn came into the kitchen and leaned against the counter. "I want to dye my hair red," she said.

"Why?" I asked, alarmed and dismayed.

"My friends said I'd look good with red hair."

"Redheads usually have pale skin and freckles," I said, as

if reason belonged in this conversation. "Your skin is olive, like mine. So red hair wouldn't look natural." By not natural, I meant that it wouldn't look good. That's how out of date I was.

"Some kids have purple hair," Jocelyn said. "Purple hair can look good on the right person."

I wondered what kind of person would look good with purple hair. I suspected Jocelyn was trying to be accepted by two girls named Amanda and Kayla who so far had only made Jocelyn miserable by teaming up against her and occasionally expelling her from the group. A few months earlier, Jocelyn's English teacher, a savvy and observant young woman, told me that for some reason, the smart clique wouldn't accept Jocelyn, so she was stuck with this group of outsiders.

To make sure, I asked, "Who else has dyed their hair?"

"Kayla."

"I thought you were an individualist," I said, trying a different angle. "I didn't think you were the type to do things just because your friends suggested it."

"Dying your hair red is individual."

"Not if kids are dying their hair purple!" I told her about a photograph and caption I remembered from the eighties: Five girls dressed to the hilt like Madonna, walking down the street with their heavy crucifix necklaces and jangling earrings, frizzy bleached hair, fire-engine red lipstick, and black lacy underwear showing under their clothes. The caption said: "In the name of individualism."

Jocelyn didn't think it was funny. "I want red hair."

"Show me what kind of red."

Jocelyn went into her room and came back with a Teen Girl magazine. She opened the magazine to an ad for a hair color called Pulse Red, a neon glow-in-the-dark red. The ad said the color washed out in eight to twelve shampoos. I assumed that part was put in for the parents.

"We have to see what Dad thinks," I said, stalling for time. I knew, and so did Jocelyn, what Eric would think. He wouldn't like it.

Suddenly Rebecca, in her crib in the bedroom, started wailing—flat-out, inexplicable, at-the-top-of-her-lungs wailing. I went to pick her up and tried to soothe her.

When Rebecca cried like this, she drew her knees up to her tummy and became red in the face. When she was particularly distressed, as she was now, she turned down the corners of her mouth the way you'd paint a sad face on a clown. Nathan called her the infant drama queen, and Jocelyn often said: "Mom, the baby's making her tragic face again."

Rebecca screamed as if she were in pain for a full ten minutes then suddenly stopped. She looked at me calmly, her eyes large and round and brown. Then, inexplicably, with something like a smile, she closed her eyes and went back to sleep.

One advantage to having both teenagers and an infant is that each age gives you a perspective on the other. Sometimes Eric and I spent upwards of fifteen minutes trying to get Rebecca to burp. Then Nathan sat down to dinner and burped, and we reprimanded him. We had trouble getting Rebecca to sleep in her own bed; we had trouble getting Jocelyn out of hers. Then there are moments when you find that an infant's colicky crying can make a teenager seem reasonable.

My cell phone rang. It was a phone number I didn't recognize. "Hello?"

"Cassie," Eric said. "I've been arrested. I'm at the police station."

"*What?*"

"I've been framed. This is humiliating. Come get me out of here. We may have to call that Howard guy."

He meant Howard Bracknell, the best criminal defense lawyer in Sacramento. I'd worked for Howard after my second year of law school.

"I'll be right over." I hung up. My hands were shaking when I put the enchiladas on the table. I told the twins they were eating on their own. I'd have to take Rebecca with me. For all I knew, this could take hours. I bundled her into a few extra blankets.

"Where are you going?" Jocelyn asked.

"I have to get Dad." I discouraged questions by moving quickly, and giving lots of instructions on clean up and bed times. They'd probably figure his car had broken down. It would never occur to them that Eric had been arrested. Not their father, who had probably never done anything wrong in his life.

I grabbed the checkbook and the spare credit cards we kept for emergencies and drove directly to the police station.

At the station, I went to the front desk and I asked for Eric Sanders. A heavy-set police officer with a closely shaved head and a grim expression told me to wait. I waited in an open area like the waiting room of a hospital emergency room with scuffed walls, glaring fluorescent lights, vending machines, and nervous people milling about. The room smelled of dust and old coffee.

Some people were sleeping in chairs. I looked at them, enviously. That was just what I wanted to do—go to sleep and wake up to find out this was all nothing more than an eerie dream, and I wasn't really in the waiting area of the county jail.

Rebecca started to fuss, so I released her from the carrier, put her on my shoulder, and paced back and forth along the back wall.

The officer with the shaved head came back and told me to follow him. So I did, carrying the empty carrier in one hand, the diaper bag slung over one shoulder, and Rebecca on the other shoulder. The officer turned to see why I was moving so slowly. He made a gesture, offering to help.

"Thanks," I said, handing him the diaper bag.

He led me to a room with several desks, each with a computer. A few officers were sitting at desks, and a few others were milling around. The officer I was following put the diaper bag on a table, turned to face me, and said: "Bail for Eric Sanders is $25,000."

$25,000? Good Lord. Did they think he committed murder?

"Do you take credit cards?" I asked, feeling foolish.

I expected him to snicker at the absurdity of the question. Instead, he said, "We do, actually. The bail bond companies hate it because they don't get a fee. But $25,000 on plastic is the quickest way out of here."

I handed him three credit cards and asked him to divide the amount roughly between them. He swiped the cards on one of those machines they have in grocery stores. Who would have thought bailing a husband out of jail would be so easy?

The problem was that the machine rejected all three credit cards, so I had to call the phone number on the back of each card and speak to a real person. Each charge had been denied because the amount was large and not part of any pattern of usage on the card. Pattern of usage? I would hope *not*. I had to speak to supervisors and give my identifying information before the amounts were approved.

After the charges went through and the machines did their clicking and receipt printing, the officer left again and came back with Eric. He held himself very straight, his lips pale and set in a thin line. Nobody but me would know how angry he was just then. The more super-controlled Eric became, the angrier he was down deep.

"Sign these papers," the officer told Eric. When Eric gripped the pen, I saw he was shaking.

The officer said, "Be at the courthouse Friday, at eleven."

Eric nodded stiffly.

The officer opened a locker on the back wall, handed Eric his wallet and keys, and pointed to the door. "You can go."

I'd parked in the front of the lot, near the building, under a street light. I opened the back door and strapped Rebecca into her car seat, then sat in the front and looked at Eric. "What happened?"

"I was at the house," Eric said, "going through the mail. A guy rang the doorbell and said he'd left his jacket at our house. He said he was with the electrical contractors and his jacket was inside. So I let him in. He walked down the hall, into the addition. He knew just where he was going. Tucked up high where the new closet will be was a rolled-up leather jacket. He took the jacket, said thanks, and left. A few minutes later, two police in uniform rang the doorbell and said they had a telephonic search warrant and were searching for methamphetamine. What the hell is a telephonic search warrant?"

"A called-in warrant. A judge is available twenty-four seven, by phone, if the police don't think they have time to get to and from the station to swear out a warrant."

Eric looked amazed. "What is this? Fast-food police procedure?"

"Something like that. Okay, so, they came in and searched."

"They searched. They opened the top drawer of my dresser, and under the socks was a baggie of white powder."

The only words that came to me had four letters. I knew from teaching high school that teenagers are extraordinarily sensitive to hypocrisy in adults, so when the twins reached fifth grade, I told Eric it was time for us to get into the habit of watching our language to set a good example. As a result, I literally could not think of a single thing to say.

"The place is wide open all day," Eric said, "with construction crews in and out, and isn't secure at night. How hard could it have been for someone to plant that jacket and the drugs?"

I assumed officers watched the guy go into the house, and I tried to visualize what the officers had seen. "So the officers saw a guy ring the doorbell, go inside, and come out with a leather jacket?"

"If someone was watching, that's what they saw. Tom has to be the one behind this. Who else? He knows the construction site. It isn't hard to figure out that I come back here every night after work to get the mail."

"Did you give the police a statement?"

"No." He gave me a look and said, "I didn't read the Mickey Mouse flashcards, but I listened to you enough to know not to do that. Did you tell the kids anything?"

"Of course not. We need to get this straightened out first. We'll call Howard tomorrow."

Jocelyn was at the kitchen table waiting for us. She saw Eric and said, "I want Pulse Red hair."

Eric blinked, startled. Naturally enough, under the circumstances, I'd forgotten to warn him about the red hair.

"They won't let you go to school with hair like that," he said.

"Yes, they will," Jocelyn said. "There are no rules about

hair."

He looked at me. I shrugged. It was only hair, after all.

"Pulse Red?" he asked. The magazine was on the counter. I opened it and I showed where the ad promised that the color washes out after eight to twelve shampoos.

He turned to Jocelyn and said, "Can I give you some advice—"

"Oh, *Dad*." She got that look that meant she was shutting down. She narrowed her eyes to slits, and turned away.

Eric looked at me, hurt. We'd both anticipated some pulling back when the twins reached adolescence, but Eric evidently was not prepared for his little girl outright rejecting his advice, unheard. To help him out, I said, "She's thirteen. You can't tell her."

"That's why we had another baby," he explained gloomily, to nobody in particular. "So I can have someone to tell."

5

Eric had a rough night. I woke up several times to find him staring at the ceiling. I snuggled into the crook of his arm. I didn't try to reassure him that everything would be all right, that surely once the D.A. understood how flimsy the evidence was, charges wouldn't be filed at all. I didn't bother because I knew he wouldn't have believed me. He would have accused me of being naive.

The next morning, after the twins went to school, I called Howard's office to make an appointment. He could see us right away. We took Rebecca to a drop-off daycare center downtown, not far from Howard's office.

Howard's office, appropriately enough, was housed in a beautiful old building with Ionic columns and flowery scrolls and the words "Justice for All" inscribed over the doorway. The building had once housed the local courthouse and now housed the city's public law library.

Howard's office, done in soothing shades of gray and pale blue, had the comforting smell of books. Lisa, who sat at the front desk, wore the kind of teased hairstyle you don't expect to see on a young woman.

"Howard is waiting for you in the conference room," Lisa said.

Howard stood up to greet us and shake our hands. He had the bearing of an old-fashioned gentleman: Tall and lanky with white hair so pale it had probably once been blond, wearing a crisp navy suit, a starched white shirt, and a red tie. The legal profession had gone casual—even lawyers in Boston reportedly went to work in casual clothes—but Howard believed a lawyer should look the part.

We sat down. "All right," he said. "What happened?"

Eric told him about hiring Tom Mullin, how he trashed the project, how we were heading toward litigation with him, and how we'd moved out of the house, and what happened the night before. "Right after the guy left with the jacket," Eric said, "the police knocked on the door and said they were searching for methamphetamine. They had a warrant so I let them in. They found a baggie of methamphetamine in my top bureau drawer."

Howard said, "You do understand that you are presumed to be in personal possession of drugs in your own home?"

"We're not living in the house," Eric said. "We moved out because of the construction, and the new baby." Eric handed him a copy of the month-to-month lease we'd signed on our apartment.

"Crews are in and out all day," I said. "Anyone can get in, any time. The new window isn't installed so it can be popped out, the crawl space isn't secure. Anyone familiar with the site willing to crawl on his belly can get into the house."

Howard looked at the lease, and asked Eric, "What were you doing at the house when you were arrested?"

"I stop by the house most days after work to pick up the mail and look around. I'm usually there ten or fifteen minutes, tops."

"So," Howard said, "you handed the jacket to the guy who

posed as a construction worker?"

"No. I never touched the jacket. He came into the house, went to the addition, reached up into the new closet, and took it down."

I felt a new surge of hope. "What about fingerprints," I said. "Eric's fingerprints won't be on the jacket, or the bags holding the drugs."

"If someone smart is behind this, the person would have used something of yours to hold the drugs, so they'll find fingerprints. Asking for fingerprints is usually a bad idea. If the D.A. doesn't look for prints, we have an opening with a jury."

"But we weren't even living there," I said. "Other people had full access."

"If you aren't living there," Howard said, "if the house isn't secure, and people are in and out all day, the case does look shaky. I'll call the D.A. Maybe they'll hold off charging a crime until they do some more investigating."

Eric put his hands flat on the table and said, "What else can I do?"

"Don't talk to anyone at all about this. Not a word. If they charge you, there may be a notice in the paper, so you may have to warn your employer."

"I hate to ask this question," Eric said, "because I'm going to figure how to prove that Tom framed me, but I want to know. What's the penalty for this?"

"Possessing and selling methamphetamine out of your home will probably get you two to five years in prison."

I knew how Eric was feeling just then: He was feeling kicked in the stomach. Eric would find it an affront to his moral integrity to be fined for littering a sidewalk.

"Will you need a retainer from us?" I asked.

"No. Lisa will sign you up. We'll give you the professional

courtesy discount for lawyers, and you won't have to pay a retainer."

During the drive home, I said to Eric, "I'm surprised a criminal defense firm has a professional discount for lawyers."

Eric shot me a look. "Why shouldn't they get a discount?"

"But do you really think there are that many lawyers who need criminal defense attorneys?"

He shot me another look and gave a cynical chuckle.

He pulled into the parking lot of a Kingsbury Coffee Shop on Broadway. Once inside, I ordered peppermint tea and he ordered a decaf. We settled into our booth. At two in the afternoon, we were the only customers in the shop. A young man was behind the counter, cleaning up.

Eric put his hands flat on the table, leaned forward, and said, "I'm thinking about hiring Big Dan to go after Tom."

"Tell me you're not serious."

"I don't know if I'm serious. Maybe it's just fantasy, but that's what I'm thinking about."

"If you do something like that, you could *really* get in trouble."

"Cassie, I'm in trouble now. If I'm going down for something I didn't do, Tom is going with me."

"Maybe you're not in trouble. Howard says it doesn't look like they have much of a case. You didn't do anything wrong, so you shouldn't have to worry."

"Cassie. The world isn't like law school and moot court. People get framed. People get convicted for things they didn't do."

"One thing I know is that police bluster and say they have more evidence than they have to scare people into confessing. We just have to wait and see. I know, it's really, really scary."

"I don't feel scared, actually. I feel pissed." Indeed, Eric was so tense he reminded me of a rubber band about to snap. Not that I blamed him. It had been bad enough before, when it just looked like our contractor had lost his marbles and left us with a mess.

"I should have Tom murdered," he said.

I looked around, even though the place was empty. "If you say anything like that again, I'm walking out."

"I'm sorry. I don't mean it." He used his 'I-must-prevent-my-wife-who-just-had-a-baby-from-having-another-crying-jag voice.

Tom's last day on the job—the day we deliberately didn't fire him—was December twenty-second. It started when Eric picked up part of the plywood floor in the addition and saw that underneath was the main water valve. We'd told Tom when we hired him that the water valve had to be relocated. You obviously can't have your main water valve under the house.

The next morning, Eric stayed home from work so that he could confront Tom. That was shortly after Rebecca's birth and I just didn't want to do it. That was one of the days nobody showed up for work, so Eric couldn't confront him either.

Tom finally showed up the next day at noon. I called Eric to tell him.

About twenty minutes later, Eric marched through the front door and went to talk to Tom. He picked up the plywood and showed Tom the water valve. Tom said, "I know. I still have to move it."

"Wouldn't it have been easier," Eric asked, speaking slowly, "to move the water valve before you built a room on top of it?"

Tom admitted that it would be much easier to relocate a water valve if a room was not built on top of it. Then he blamed his incompetent crew, who he had long since fired. Then he started to whine. "My back has been hurting," he said. "I've had to go three times to a chiropractor. I've been working my ass off for you."

"I believe that," said Eric. "But working hard doesn't always mean working smart." Eric, despite his anger, could make a very reasonable statement like "Working hard doesn't always mean working smart."

"When are you planning to move the water valve?" Eric asked.

"Kristin and I will move it today."

"Don't you think you should bring in a professional plumber?"

"There's nothing to moving a water valve," Tom said. "I can do it."

By then, of course, we had serious doubts about whether he could do it. But I wasn't ready to fire him—at the time I still believed the room would get built quicker with Tom on the job, than if we had no contractor at all.

At about four o'clock I bundled up the baby, put her in the stroller, and went out for a walk. When I returned, Kristin and Tom were gone. I lifted the plywood to see what they had done.

What they had done, unbelievably, was piece together more than thirty pieces of pipe, each no more than two or three inches long, of all different sizes, into a maze of pipe. The final product looked like a half dozen bent bagpipes welded together. The piping made a number of twists and full turns before going through a hole Tom had drilled in the external wall. It looked like the kind of maze a scientist might use to see if a mouse would get confused trying to get from one opening to the other.

In the bathroom I found a note taped to the mirror. It was from Kristin: "Sorry that the water is turned off," she had written. "Tom will be back later tonight to get it turned on again."

I opened the tap, and sure enough, the water was off. When Eric got home, he turned on the main water valve, now located on the side of the addition. With the water turned on, water sprayed in several places from Tom's contraption. With water spraying from several joints, the thing looked like a bizarre fountain.

Eric turned off the water and went to the neighbor's to get a few jugs of tap water. We waited to hear from Tom, but he never called or showed up. Eric tried to call him but his cell phone voice mailbox was full and not accepting new messages. Eric went online and found a phone number and address for "T & K Mullin." Tom's wife's name was Kelly.

Eric called the number and asked for Tom. A woman answered and said: "Nobody named Tom lives here," and hung up.

The next morning at eleven o'clock Kristin showed up. I asked her why Tom hadn't come back to get our water working. She said she left a message for him at his chiropractor's office, but he said he didn't get the message. "I called this morning but Kelly, his wife, said Tom had to take Buddy to the vet."

"Watch out," I told her. "If you work for Tom Mullin, he'll end up blaming you for everything."

"Oh, no," she said earnestly. "Tom's just had a hard time hiring decent people. He's really been working hard to get the job done."

I pointed to the plumbing apparatus. "Does that look right to you?"

"Well—" she said, uncertainly.

"Remember that I warned you," I said. I brought her a pitcher of water and a glass, and went back to the front of the house and closed the door.

Tom did not show up that day. At five o'clock Kristin went home. A six o'clock Eric and I packed some clothes and checked the family into a hotel. That night, Eric and I came up with a proposal, a way to get the project finished and to keep Tom on the job. Our idea was for Tom to continue hiring and supervising the roofing, stucco, and other subcontractors—all of whom had done work that looked fine, until they mysteriously stopped working—and we would hire plumbers and electricians to do the work Tom had been trying unsuccessfully to do himself.

The next day at about one, Tom and Kristin showed up and worked all afternoon. When they finished at about six, the water was on.

After they left, I went into the backyard and saw that Tom's toolbox was gone. In fact, all Tom's personal things—ladders, tools, tarps—were also gone.

That was the last we heard from him, until Paula Armstrong called and demanded to know when he could come back to finish the project.

The morning after Tom left, his plumbing contraption was damp with droplets of water. By the second day, there were full leaks in two places. The wonder was that it wasn't leaking in more places. Eric called Tom, reached his voicemail, and left several messages. When three days passed without a response, we called a plumber recommended by a neighbor. The plumber said he'd never in his life seen a contraption like that. It took him eight hours to replace Tom's piping with a clean, elegant, and professional looking pipe, and another afternoon to get the sprinklers tied in to the new system. The bill came to over eleven hundred dollars.

We saved Tom's plumbing contraption. Just before we moved into our apartment, we had some neighbors over for coffee and cake so we could explain where we would be, and to ask them to keep an eye on the house. I guess we wanted some sympathy because we showed them Tom's contraption.

One neighbor looked at Tom's contraption and asked, "If you blow through it, can you hear Taps?"

6

Jocelyn's hair didn't turn out so badly, partly because her hair didn't match the neon color on the package. The actual color was a deep auburn, which, against her golden-hued skin and deep brown eyes, looked interesting rather than completely wrong. It also wasn't so bad in the sense that a stranger glancing at her wouldn't automatically think, "Who's that weird kid?" Even if it wasn't quite the neon color she envisioned, she was pleased with it, you could tell. She spent a half hour each morning on her hair, first straightening it (over the past year, her hair had developed a few waves) and then curling the ends just right.

It was early Friday, just after the twins left for school but before Eric left for work, when Howard called. Eric put him on speaker phone. "Me and Cassie are both here."

"I have some good news," Howard said. "I persuaded the D.A. to do some further investigating before he files charges. So Eric doesn't have to show up at the courthouse at eleven. The rest of the news is bad. Apparently the cops have a cell phone with a message they say Eric left. The phone call was made from your house phone. They're claiming Eric said he'd have the package at his house between 6:00 and 6:30."

"Anyone could make a call from my house phone!" Eric

said. "People are in and out all day! I'm only there to pick up the mail after work."

"I explained that to the D.A. We can ask them to do a voice analysis, but Eric, you need to think about whether you want to do that. If it's your voice, it's all over. We'll have no defense."

"Can someone record me talking and doctor it up?"

"I suppose so. I'd think an expert would be able to tell, but that means bringing in experts. If we can find an expert willing to say it was doctored, they can find an expert willing to say it wasn't. Asking for a voice analysis might make our job harder."

"I want the voice analysis," Eric said.

I felt unsettled, remembering the many phone messages he had left for Tom during Tom's last days on the job when the situation was rapidly deteriorating.

"I'll set up a time for you to go in for the analysis," Howard said.

After Eric hung up the phone, I said, "Are you sure a voice analysis is a good idea?"

"I don't see the risk. I don't think Tom is competent enough to figure out how to splice together voice recordings."

He had a point there. Look at how Tom spliced together plumbing pipes.

"Maybe Tom hired someone competent to frame you."

"He had a hard time hiring someone competent enough to install a door knob. You give him way too much credit."

It seemed to me it was better to give him too much credit than not enough credit. Not that I wanted to take life's lessons from the Godfather, but wasn't it a good idea in this situation to overestimate your friends and underestimate your enemies?

Howard's assistant called back and told Eric to meet Howard at the police station later that afternoon. I asked Eric if he wanted me to go with him, and he said no, he'd be fine.

"I may as well go to work until then," he said.

The city inspectors gave me a list of approved structural engineers. I selected one with particularly good references and emailed him photographs of the hold-downs. Within a few hours, he sent me an email telling me the hold-downs needed to be redrilled so that they were straight.

I found Paula Armstrong's email address on the California Bar Association web page. That's when I found out that she had attended a well-respected local law school ten years earlier. She appeared to be a solo practitioner. Her office was in an older building in the downtown area.

I emailed her the photographs and a copy of the engineer's message telling us that the hold-downs had to be drilled straight.

She wrote back immediately. "You have to let Tom back on the property to make the repairs. He will not pay the bill if you hire someone else to do the work. You have a contract with him."

Yeah, right, I thought. As if Tom was capable of drilling anything straight.

The twins arrived home from school at the usual time. The sight of Jocelyn was a fresh surprise. Where was my daughter with the lovely honey-colored hair?

"What did the kids say about your hair?" I asked her.

She gave a disgusted look. "Kids keep coming up to me and saying, 'Did you dye your hair?' Like, duh. What do they think?"

"Not a particularly insightful question," I said.

"I started giving answers like: 'No! I didn't dye it! I woke up in the morning and it was red! Did that ever happen to you?'"

We both laughed.

When Eric walked in the door, I told him what Paula had said.

"Okay," Eric said. "Let's tell that Paula person that Tom can redrill the hold-downs if he does it by tomorrow at noon."

"What if he gets there by noon?" I asked.

"He won't. When has he ever gotten anywhere by noon?"

So Eric wrote back and told Paula Armstrong that Tom could make the repairs if he did so by the next day, at noon.

"Let's hope he doesn't make it," I said.

"He won't make it," Eric said.

At eleven the next morning, I logged into our email account and found a message from Paula Armstrong:

> *Tom will not be coming to fix the hold-downs. I've reviewed some documents that show the city has already inspected the hold-downs, and signed off on them. So I don't really understand what the problem is, since the city has signed off on everything. Let me know if you have any questions. Paula Armstrong.*

Amazed, I scanned and emailed her copies of the correction notices. She wrote back, "These must not be genuine."

My first year civil procedure professor once said, "Be careful who you represent, because you will become like your clients." He talked about how everyone knows that people pick dogs that are like them—fluffy-haired people like fluffy dogs, mean people like attack dogs. He said, "The same is true of lawyers and clients. Clients pick lawyers who are like them, or who can become like them."

I wondered what Paula Armstrong would do when she found out—as she no doubt would—that her client was a lying sack.

I called the first contractor we had spoken to, the one who had done a lot of work in our neighborhood, the one who had told us "anyone can do this job." He'd recently put an entire second story on a house down the block. At the corner market, I'd seen Grace, the homeowner, who told me he was "brilliant, but arrogant." He'd done all the work in seven weeks.

I called the brilliant but arrogant contractor, reminded him who I was, and told him I was in a real bind. When I explained the situation—a new baby and a house torn apart and a contractor's nightmare—he felt sorry for me. He said that on Wednesday he had a break in his schedule. He'd meet me at the house Wednesday morning with a few workers to redrill the hold-downs so that they were straight. The charge would be five hundred dollars.

Wednesday morning, when his workers tried to drill the bolts straight down, they hit air. Nothing. There was no foundation directly under the frame to drill into. The contractor showed me that if you looked down, you could see that the foundation had been poured in the wrong place, and that the frame was hanging off the foundation. The only way to get the bolt to reach from the frame to the foundation was to bend it into the shape of an "S," which explained why Tom had in fact bent the bolt. This also meant Tom had known that the bolt couldn't be drilled straight, which might explain why he hadn't come to fix it when we'd given him the chance.

"You got more serious problems here than you realize," he said, a comment that didn't strike me as particularly arrogant or brilliant.

7

When the Sacramento County Recorder's Office sends you a notice, you know right away from the weight of the envelope and the official stamp on the return address that the envelope contains something important. I had no idea what we could be receiving from the County Recorder's Office.

Inside, astonishingly enough, was a notice that Mullin Construction had put a mechanic's lien on our house. I had to read the document three times before I believed that it was not a practical joke.

I reached for my cell phone. My hands were shaking.

Fortunately, Eric answered right away. "You won't believe this," I said.

He must have heard the shock and urgency in my voice, because he said, "What's the matter, Cassie? Are you all right?"

"I'm fine. Tom put a lien on our house."

"*What?*"

"A mechanic's lien."

"This is getting weirder and weirder," he said. "What does he say we owe him?"

"All it says is, 'contract price plus extra work.'"

"He's out of his mind," said Eric. "He never did any extra work."

I didn't say anything.

"Cassie?"

"What about the Tree Guy?"

"Don't even *think* about that incident. It's over and done with, and Tom wouldn't dare try to make something out of it."

Rebecca started wailing so I had to hang up.

When someone tells you not to think about something, what do you generally do? That's right, you think about it. And that was just what I did.

The incident with the tree service guy, in late September, started innocently enough. It was a Thursday and Tom's crew had arrived for work at about nine, but Tom was nowhere around. I was in my eighth month of pregnancy, and generally tried to ignore what was happening with the construction. But whenever I looked outside, I saw a half dozen men idling around the backyard.

Tom never showed up that day, but evidently he spoke to one guy, who I came to think of as the Tree Guy. The Tree Guy knocked on the back door at about two o'clock and told me that Tom had instructed him to remove the small redwoods in the back of the house. For some reason, the owners before us had planted redwoods within a few feet of the house—not very sensible considering that in time the roots would overturn the house. The redwoods were just a foot or so taller than me, so they could still be easily removed. When we'd hired Tom, Eric had said, "I'll dig up those redwoods before you start building." Tom had asked, instead, if he could have them. He said he had a perfect place for them on his property. "They're nice looking redwoods," Tom had said. Eric said he was welcome to them.

So when this guy, who was large and blond and wore a white tank top, knocked on my backdoor and said he was going to remove the redwoods, I said fine.

Some time later the guy knocked on the door again and told me he'd gotten rid of the redwoods. He said, "Tom told me to see if you need any tree work done. He said I may as well do it, since I'm just hanging around here."

In fact, I'd been worried about two of our branches that hung over the sidewalk. Our contract with Tom specified that extra work would be billed at $60 an hour. I showed the Tree Guy those branches and asked if trimming the ones hanging over the sidewalk would take more than two hours. He said about two hours. So I said he could trim the branches. He spent two hours trimming the two branches so that they were no longer dangling dangerously over the sidewalk.

Four days later Tom knocked at the back door and handed me an invoice for tree service work. The charge for pulling out the redwoods was $250. The charge for trimming the branches was $600.

The invoice was not one of Tom's; it was a tree service invoice with a tree logo printed at the top. I felt suddenly shaky. I wished Eric were here to handle this. My emotional responses were intensified because of my advanced pregnancy. I was disoriented. The only thing I could think to say was, "Eric was going to pull out the redwoods, but you told him you wanted them."

Tom looked thoughtful. He reached for a pen from the patio table and drew a line through the charge of $250 for pulling out the redwoods. "There is no charge for this," he said. He left the $600 charge for trimming branches.

$600 for one guy working two hours was outrageous. What I thought, in my confusion, was that the Tree Guy had scammed me by posing as one of Tom's workers.

"Is he licensed?" I asked, reaching for the invoice to see

if a license number was printed there. Tom stepped back and looked at the invoice. He said, "I don't know if he's licensed." He sounded concerned, and then folded the invoice and put it in his pocket. I was so deeply rattled that it didn't occur to me until later that he had deliberately prevented me from keeping the invoice.

My voice was shaking when I said, "He's trying to overcharge me. The contract says $60 for extra work. Whoever heard of three hundred dollars an hour for trimming trees!"

"Hmm." Tom looked toward his feet instead of at me. When he left, I assumed he was going to confront the Tree Guy and find out what had happened.

Tom never mentioned the $600 tree service charge again. Eric believed that Tom, not the Tree Guy, had been scamming us. Eric also believed that Tom had dropped the whole thing when he saw that the scam didn't work.

Eric walked in from work and said, "Let's go out here," and gestured to the patio door.

I picked up Rebecca and followed him outside. Once the door closed behind us, Eric whispered, "Howard called. He got more discovery from the D.A. They say the call I supposedly made from the house was made at six fifteen, the time I usually stop by to pick up the mail."

"They can't prove anything from that," I said.

"Cassie. I'm starting to think Tom isn't the one framing me."

"Who else could it be?"

"I don't know. But Tom isn't this smart."

8

Jocelyn came out of the bathroom the next morning and sat down at the kitchen table wearing startlingly heavy black eye makeup. It was hard not to stare. Because black was smeared under both eyes, it looked like she had smeared it on purpose. Her eyes looked bruised. Eric and I exchanged glances.

Nathan looked up, did a double take when he saw Jocelyn's face, and then went on eating his cereal. Nathan can go either way at a moment like that. He can say something mocking to start an uproar, or he can ignore the situation. Fortunately just then he was in the mood to ignore.

Eric drove the kids to school. After he dropped them off, he called and said, "I didn't say anything." He said this with as much pride as he might have announced that he'd successfully climbed Mount Everest. "I figured you should handle it."

"I'll find a good time to tell her that she'd look better if the makeup wasn't so heavy."

If I could forbid Jocelyn to wear makeup, I would. If I could forbid her to have a boyfriend until she was twenty, I'd do that too. If I could keep her in my sight for the next six years, until she was safely through adolescence, I'd do that as well. But I feared that such extremes backfire. I'd rather see what she was doing than have her go underground. At the same time, nobody looks good with such heavy black makeup and I thought I should tell her. On the other hand, what did I know about what was considered good looking in middle school? When the standard of beauty includes purple and Pulse Red hair and yellow spikes, the ideal in eye makeup is anyone's guess.

I stopped by the house for the mail, and there was a letter from Paula Armstrong. The return address on the envelope had been stamped with a preprinted ink stamp. I opened the envelope, curious. The main paragraph stated:

> *On December 22 you told Tom Mullin to pack up his tools and leave your property. You have refused to let him back since. I am writing to notify you that if you hire any independent third parties to complete the job, you will be in breach of the contract. Pursuant to your contract, Mullin Construction will be entitled to reimbursement for all work done to date plus ten percent of the contract price.*

I kept the contract in a file in a box in the kitchen. I drove back to the apartment to check the contract to see if what she was saying about the ten percent was true. In fact, the contract stated that the homeowner would be liable for ten percent of the contract price, as a cancellation fee, if the owner canceled the contract without cause or justification. Paula seemed to have overlooked the entire clause following the word "if."

The next day brought a letter from Tom Mullin as irritating as the one from Paula. Tom wrote:

*On December 22 you requested that I remove all
materials and tools from the job site located at 3931
River Park Drive. You stated that you would contact
me after you decided how to proceed with Mullin
Construction. I am ready and waiting to complete the
job. You have 72 hours from the date of this letter to
contact me with your decision.*

Among the bizarre aspects of this letter—besides, of
course, the blatant lies and threat—was that he had our address
wrong.

During the last week of January, I was assigned my first case.
My client was Tremaine Carter, a sixteen-year-old convicted
of carjacking. What happened was that at about eight p.m.,
a gentleman named Roberto parked his car in a gas station
parking lot. He crossed a divider and a grassy patch and was
talking on his phone when Tremaine and a friend named Jerry
approached him. Jerry, whose hands were in his pants pockets,
pointed his index finger to look as if he had a gun in his pants.
He said, "Throw my friend the keys to your car."

Roberto told the boys his keys were already in the car, on
the seat. Tremaine and Jerry went to the car, found the keys,
and drove away.

Tremaine and Jerry were picked up by the police at one
a.m. when they drove Roberto's car through a residential area
making a terrible rattle. What they'd done, evidently, in the
intervening hours, was so thoroughly bang up the car that
something underneath rattled and clanked. The rattling alerted
local residents, who called the police.

Tremaine was convicted of carjacking. I was appointed by
the court to write his appeal.

You may wonder what I could possibly do for Tremaine.

You may also wonder why I would want to do anything for him. What I did was some hairsplitting: I argued that he should have been convicted of car theft instead of carjacking, a less serious offense, because the victim wasn't in or right near the car when it was stolen.

I suppose there's a certain irony and call for introspection whenever a criminal defense type becomes the victim of a crime.

Later that day, I had just returned from the grocery store and was standing in front of the apartment door fumbling for my keys when someone behind me called out sharply, "Cassie?"

I turned to face a young man wearing jeans and a white tee shirt. He tried to hand me a manila envelope. Startled, I took a step back.

He said, "You are served," and dropped the envelope at my feet and left.

I watched him walk away, then picked up the envelope. Once I was inside, I locked the door behind me, put Rebecca on a blanket on the floor, and opened the envelope.

Anyone who has ever been sued knows that the documents are almost as frightening as a criminal charge. In California the notice says in big bold letters: "You are being sued," and then goes on to warn that if you do not follow the correct procedures, "your wages, money, and property may be taken without further warning from the court." You are then advised to contact an attorney right away.

According to the documents, Tom Mullin—through his attorney Paula Armstrong—was suing me and Eric, in Superior Court, for breach of contract, claiming $28,327.31 in damages.

I sat on the couch. Rebecca watched me with large round eyes. I reached for my phone and called Eric. "We've been served," I told him, and started reading the document.

"Wait a minute," Eric said. "Is this a joke?"

"This is not a joke. The complaint says we owe Tom the balance of the contract, a cancellation fee, and extra work totaling $28,327.31.

I suspected Eric was doing the arithmetic. Sure enough, the next thing he said was, "Even if they're claiming ten percent of the contract price, it leaves almost ten thousand dollars in extra work."

"It just occurred to me," I said, "they're suing us in Superior Court. The contract has a binding arbitration clause. What is Paula doing?"

"She's stupid, and he's crazy. That's all there is to that."

I skimmed a few pages and said, "They're suing to foreclose on our house."

"That scumbag," said Eric. "At least *we* should have gotten the satisfaction of serving *him* with those papers. We're going to nail his ass, Cassie."

Once, when the twins were two years old, Eric and I strapped them into their double stroller and walked to the neighborhood bakery for breakfast. The twins liked sitting in regular chairs instead of high chairs or booster chairs, so we couldn't strap them in, so they were always squirming around, sometimes squirming onto the floor. Having pastries for breakfast at the bakery was at times like coordinating a circus act.

That Sunday we arrived at the bakery and selected a table. The chair I sat in broke. A wooden piece holding the chair together cracked and the chair sort of crumbled. There was a clattering and I slid to the floor. Eric helped me up, and an employee removed the broken chair.

Nathan just watched, but Jocelyn started crying. Eric

borrowed a chair from the next table. I was unhurt, but Jocelyn wouldn't stop crying. Between sobs, she said, "Chair broken, chair broken." She kept this up all through breakfast. Before we left, she asked where the broken chair had gone. Eric told her it was in the back. She asked if someone was going to fix it, and Eric said he didn't think it could be fixed given the way the wood had cracked and splintered. I told her not to worry, it could probably be fixed. Eric shot me a look, not understanding why I had contradicted him.

When we got home, Jocelyn brought me a piece of paper and a brown crayon that was approximately the color of the chair and asked me to draw a picture of the broken chair. I drew a chair for her. Jocelyn carried the picture around with her all day. Later that afternoon, when a neighbor came to borrow our wheelbarrow, Jocelyn showed him the drawing and told him about the broken chair.

Eric, embarrassed, said, "She's fixated." You could see he was bewildered.

After the neighbor left, I told Eric, "Jocelyn's not worried about the chair. She's worried about herself. If a chair can break, just like that, and be carried away, all's not well in the world. What other things might break?"

"Or maybe she has an abnormal fixation with broken chairs."

Eric could be so literal. I said, "A little Keats wouldn't have hurt you."

"A little *what?*"

"Keats. Wordsworth. Shelley. The romantic poets who wrote about a child's first sense of evil and death. Really, business majors should be required to read poetry."

Eric gave me the look that said, "What are you talking about?"

56

For days, Jocelyn talked about the broken chair. Eric hid the drawing when she wasn't paying attention, hoping she'd stop obsessing, but the next Sunday, when we went back to the bakery, she went around and checked all the chairs to make sure none would break. Nathan, who was a late bloomer and more literal, didn't have a similar experience until the twins were four and his pet turtle died.

I put the complaint and summons into a manila folder. Occasionally through the afternoon I took the complaint and summons out of the folder and looked at them, feeling the way Jocelyn must have felt with her drawing of the broken chair.

9

I was cooking spaghetti for dinner when my cell phone vibrated. It was Eric, who I hadn't heard from all afternoon.

"Guess where I am," he said.

It was six o'clock, so, feeling hopeful, I said, "You're on your way home."

"Not a very imaginative guess," he said. I was surprised to hear something other than doom in his voice. "I'm over at the Snowden's house. Wait until you hear this."

"Eric, stop it. Who are the Snowdens?" I never enjoyed suspense.

"Remember that sample I saw of Tom's work? The project he was finishing up over by the freeway? It's been bugging me how he did such good work. Now I know. Can you come over for a few minutes?"

"Tell me."

"It's a long story. You'll never believe it. First, I'll tell you this: I called Mark to tell him what happened so he won't recommend Tom anymore, and Mark has been fired."

Mark was the draftsperson who had initially recommended Tom. Eric said, "The guy I talked to told me that Mark took money from contractors to recommend them."

"Tom paid for recommendations?"

"Yup. I was fooled twice."

"What was the other time?"

"I'll tell you when you get here. Just get in the car, and come to 136 Jeremy Way."

"All right. But you can't tell anyone about—"

"I know. I haven't."

I put my cell phone in my purse, turned off the stove, told the twins I'd be back soon, and put Rebecca in her car seat. Jeremy Way was about two miles from the apartment, toward the park. I found Eric's car in the driveway of a modest ranch-style home. I carried Rebecca up to the front door, and rang the doorbell.

A dark-haired, youngish woman—at first glance she seemed to be in her early thirties, but on closer look, maybe older—opened the door, still dressed for the office. Her face was heart-shaped and sweet, her eyes large and brown.

"You must be Cassie. Oh, my God. Come in." And then, as if an afterthought: "I'm Gina Snowden."

Rebecca opened her eyes and made a whiny noise. I gave her a pacifier.

Gina led me down a short corridor that opened to a neat and comfortable living room. Through the living room was a high-ceilinged family room. I guessed the family room to be the addition. Eric was sitting in the family room at the kind of table intended for family games with a man who I took to be Gina's husband.

"Sit down, please," Gina said in her quiet breathy voice. Then she said, "Here is Good Tom."

My heart gave a thump and I looked around.

Gina smiled. "Sorry to startle you. My husband's name is also Tom. So now I call him Good Tom so nobody gets confused."

"I've been Good Tom for almost a year now," her husband said. He had one of those calm faces that always seem to be smiling.

"You'll never believe this," Eric said after I sat down at the table. He turned to Gina and said, "Tell her."

Earnestly Gina told me, "Tom Mullin wasn't supposed to be on our property last June."

All three of them looked at me as if I was supposed to grasp the significance of this. I blinked and waited, feeling stupid.

"Uh, Cassie," Eric said. "That's when Tom brought me here to show me his work. He took me into that bathroom," Eric pointed to a bathroom just down the corridor. "He showed me the cabinets he had built in that bathroom and the flooring and tile work he had done. Then he took me over there and showed me that breakfast nook."

I still wasn't getting it.

Gina said, "He never did any work in that bathroom or breakfast nook. We had that done five years ago, with a different contractor. His last day here was in January. He left the place a mess." Then she added: "Oh my God."

"By the time I got here in June," Eric said, "Gina's brother-in-law had fixed everything."

"He duped you?" I asked Eric. "What about the work crew that was here? What about the construction?"

"Looks like it was all staged," said Eric. "A set up. A con job." He sat very straight in his chair.

I was amazed. Eric was not gullible. In fact, if there was anyone who could not be fooled, it was Eric. He was practical, and cynical, and suspicious. If Tom could fool him, then Tom could fool anyone. I tried to adjust my thinking to see Tom as a con artist instead of meek and a little stupid.

"How did Tom Mullin get into your house in June?" I asked.

"He still had a key," Gina said. "We had been asking for it back, but he never returned it. Kelly kept saying he'd return it soon, but he didn't. He knows our work schedule."

No wonder Gina kept repeating 'Oh, my God.'

"He's a smooth liar," said Eric. "I bought the whole thing."

"I can't believe he brought people here when we weren't home," Gina said. "It's creepy. It's scary. I'm calling my sister."

"Her sister is a deputy district attorney," Good Tom explained.

"Here in Sacramento?" I asked, looking at Eric.

"No, my sister works in Woodland."

"The D.A. can probably get him on trespass," I said. "Maybe even fraud."

"That's what it was," Eric said, slapping the table. "It was fraud."

I didn't know how much Eric had told them about our situation, so I said, "He trashed our house and he's claiming we owe him money."

"That's his game," said Good Tom. "His M.O. He's claiming we owe him $100,000."

"Are you the family who is friends with his wife's family?"

"That's us," said Gina. "My grandfather and Kelly's grandfather played professional basketball together. Our families have been friends for three generations."

"He told me about you guys," I said, "last September. He said you owed him $40,000."

"That was last September," said Good Tom. "Every six months or so, the amount he's demanding doubles."

"Would you mind if I took a witness statement?" I asked.

Gina and Good Tom looked at each other, startled.

"You see!" said Gina. "Getting witness statements never occurred to me. We never did anything like that. Eric told us that you documented everything and had city inspectors come and write reports. That was smart."

"Eric even made a video," I said. "It's great. Every week, on Monday, he walked around the site with a video camera, narrating as he went, saying things like, 'I don't think those wires on the ground are supposed to be in a big tangle.'"

"I wish I had thought of making a video," said Gina.

A computer was set up on a corner table. I said, "How about if you talk, and I type what you say. Is that okay? You can read it over and fix it up."

"Sure," said Gina. Good Tom turned on the computer. While we waited for it to boot up, Gina said, "You can't imagine how painful this has been for us. Sometimes I just have to have one of my sisters over here, so we sit with a glass of wine and so I can cry. We thought Tom Mullin was a friend."

The computer booted up. Good Tom opened a word processor. I pulled a chair to the computer and asked, "Is that why you hired him?"

Gina said, "We didn't meet Tom Mullin until after Kelly married him, just a few years ago. Kelly and Bad Tom's daughter Ashley and our son Sammy were born just a few months apart. Kelly knew I was taking a year off work to take care of Sammy, so she asked if I'd provide daycare for Ashley, too, so that she could work. She has an office job in an insurance company. When Kelly told me that her husband had just gotten his contractor's license, I wanted to hire him, to give him a chance, to give him his start and his first job. Then that guy, Craig something—"

"Craig Ellis," said Good Tom.

"That's right," said Gina. "Craig Ellis called me and warned me not to hire Tom Mullin. Craig said Tom had done five thousand dollars worth of damage to his kitchen. But I didn't listen because I wanted to help out Kelly's husband. So we hired him anyway." She shook her head at her own stupidity, and then said, "Oh my God, it's been horrible."

Good Tom said, "After one of Tom's workers quit, he came to warn us. He said that Tom was taking advantage of us. He also told us that Tom sometimes paid his workers with methamphetamine instead of cash."

At the word methamphetamine, I stopped typing and looked at Eric. "I guess that explains the quality of his work," I said.

"It might explain a lot of things," Eric said.

"Bad Tom and his workers did a lot of partying," Gina said, "right here in our house. One time we were gone for the weekend, and when we came back, we found beer cans in the living room and a dirty condom in our bedroom. It was *disgusting.*"

"When Tom told me you owed him forty thousand dollars," I said, "he said that you changed everything in the plans."

At the time, it hadn't occurred to me to doubt Tom's story that the clients had changed everything in the plans, causing him dozens of hours of extra work. That was back when I believed that things Tom said were at least approximately true.

"We didn't change anything in the plans!" Gina said. "He kept changing the plans. See that wooden bar with the initials? Bad Tom kept telling us we should put in a bar. We told him no, we didn't want one. My husband said that we couldn't afford to pay any more than the agreed-on price. Bad Tom talked to me in private and said he wanted to give it to my husband as a gift. At first I said no, but he kept insisting he wanted to give it as a gift, so I let him put it in. In August, after he'd been gone for eight months and we had paid fifteen thousand dollars to fix all his mistakes and finish his work, that lawyer of his called and said we owed $10,000 for the bar."

"Was the lawyer Paula Armstrong?"

"Yes," said Good Tom. "That's her name."

Eric said, "I don't understand how Tom is claiming you owe him more than $100,000."

Gina said, "Thirty thousand is because Bad Tom says we only paid him $20,000 on the contract. But we paid him $50,000. His lawyer called and told us that we'd only paid $20,000. So we went to the bank and got copies of the canceled checks totaling $50,000, and sent them to her."

"That should have shown that you paid him $50,000," I said.

Gina gave me a look. "Wait until you hear this. She called back and said his signatures had been forged. The signatures on those checks looked just like all his other signatures, but she said they were forged."

"Wait a minute," I said. "She was implying that you forged the signatures and kept the money?"

"She didn't imply it," said Good Tom. "She outright accused us of forging his signature and keeping the money."

"Wow," I said. "Did Tom or Paula go to the police?"

"No, they didn't," said Gina. "I wish they would. The police would investigate and see that we hadn't forged anything and that would be the end of it. We went back to the bank and asked about the checks Tom said we'd forged, and listen to this. The bank told us that all that money had been taken out in cash. Cash! $30,000 in cash."

"The transactions have to be on tape," I said. "A bank is not going to hand over that kind of cash without plenty of identification. It seems to me that if Paula Armstrong really believed that you, or someone else, defrauded the bank and her client out of $30,000, she would have had Tom report it to the police."

"Speaking of the police," Good Tom said, "did you know that Tom Mullin has a criminal record?"

"No," I said, more in dismay than denial. "What for?"

"We don't know," said Gina. "Only that he has one. One of his workers said he bragged about his prison time. Then my mother said Kelly's family knows something about it. I asked my sister to look it up to see what he did, but she said she's not supposed to."

"I can find out," I said. To Eric, I said, "We thought we'd been so careful, going on the draftsperson's recommendation, checking to make sure his license was valid, looking at a sample of his work. It never occurred to us to check his criminal record."

"Who would think of that?" Gina said kindly. "We certainly didn't. Some people don't even check for a license. I never heard of anyone doing a criminal check before hiring a contractor."

"I remember the day I saw this house," Eric said. "Later I thought I should come back and knock on the door and talk to the homeowners, but I figured talking to his work crew and seeing their work was enough. Boy was I stupid."

"You?" Gina said. "You weren't stupid. You took pictures. You made videos. You documented the mistakes. We didn't do any of that. We thought we'd just fix his errors to keep peace between the families. I don't even think we ever signed a contract with him. We looked but can't find one, and we may not have signed anything. We never got a permit or inspections. He didn't mention it, and it never occurred to us. Think how stupid we're going to look at a trial."

It seemed to me that not getting the permit and inspections made Tom look bad, not the Snowdens.

"The thing is," said Gina, "if he would have just asked me for another ten thousand dollars, I would have given it to him. But he didn't ask for anything at all until after he stopped coming to work and we paid all that money to fix his mistakes, and then he started making irrational demands for money!"

Of all the things that Gina had just said, what most astonished me was that she would have just given Tom another ten thousand dollars, if he had asked.

"It's easy to see why he's suing you for so much more than he's suing us," I said.

"Yes, it is," said Gina, "because you're smarter."

"No," I said, "because you're nicer. We wouldn't have given him an extra ten thousand dollars if we didn't think we owed it."

"Never," Eric agreed.

"At some point," I said, "he must have seen his game wasn't going to work with us."

"He's not used to getting so much resistance," Gina said. "I'd worry he might do something desperate."

Eric and I looked at each other.

Gina walked to a corner of the room and said, "Come look at this." She lifted a rug to show us the haphazard patchwork of floor underneath.

"Yup," said Eric. "That's Tom Mullin's signature. I'd recognize his work anywhere."

"We fixed everything else," Gina said, "But you can see how completely weird his work started to look." Then she said, "The lesson is, don't give your kids too much money. If kids feel too entitled, this is what happens."

Gina must have seen my puzzlement, because she said, "I

guess you don't know anything about Bad Tom's family."

"Nothing at all," I said.

"His family has a lot of money. All of his life, they've been bailing him out of trouble. Now he's been cut off. His sisters won't have anything to do with him. Kelly's mother told my mother that Tom's mother said she's had it, if he lands in jail again, he can just stay there."

Now I had to do another mental adjustment to imagine Tom coming from family money. But then, if Kelly's grandfather had played professional basketball, the obvious occurred to me. "Does Kelly's family have money, too?"

"Oh yes," said Gina. "Her parents just sold a business in San Francisco for a few million dollars."

I had always thought Kelly and Tom seemed like an odd couple. Tom was tall, good looking in a boyish way, and had a natural charm. I'd seen his charm myself, and besides, nothing else accounted for his ability to lure people in and con them. Kelly, in contrast, was small and very quiet.

"He always sent Kelly to give us invoices and ask us for checks," I said.

"He definitely uses her that way," said Gina. "She even called us once and told us we should pay Tom the money we owe him. Last month her family got hopeful that she was going to leave him. Kelly and Tom had a big blow out and she said she was going to look for her own apartment and leave him. She even asked her parents to help take care of her kids for a few weeks while she tried to get herself another place to live, but by the end of the month, she was back with him."

Rebecca started fussing. It was getting late. The twins would soon be hungry—if Nathan wasn't already raiding the refrigerator.

I thought of something else I wanted to know. "What

happened to the guy who called to warn you? The one with the five thousand dollars worth of damage in his kitchen?"

"He ended up paying Tom another five thousand dollars to get rid of him," Gina said. "When Craig first called us, he thought it was all over. He thought that all he had to do was pay to correct the mistakes and he'd be done. He had no idea Tom was going to come after him. At least he was smart enough to document the damage before he fixed everything."

"If he documented the damage," I asked, "why did he pay five thousand dollars?"

"Bad Tom's lawyer, that Paula Armstrong person, wrote Craig a nasty letter about how he still owed Tom money. Craig hired a lawyer, and his lawyer said Craig had a good case, but the damages he could collect wouldn't be worth the legal bills he'd have to pay. So he settled by giving Tom five thousand dollars to go away. Craig felt cheated twice, once when Tom trashed his kitchen, then when he had to pay five thousand dollars to get rid of a lawsuit."

No wonder Tom's game usually worked. If Gina was willing to give him another ten thousand dollars for the asking, and Craig paid five thousand dollars to get rid of him—if money could come that easily, why do a good job?

What I didn't understand was why Paula was doing this. Did she realize she was helping a criminal? Was she in on the deal? Or had he fooled her into believing that we were all taking advantage of poor Tom?

"What gets me," I said, "is that none of this would work without Paula Armstrong. He needs a lawyer willing to call his victims and demand money."

"Exactly," said Eric. "What I'd like to know is the difference between that, and extortion."

He looked at me. Everyone waited to see what I would say.

This made sense. It was a legal question, and I was the lawyer.

"Well, let's see," I said, speaking slowly because I was inventing as I went along. It hurt to admit the truth, but I said: "The difference between that and extortion is that Paula Armstrong is a licensed and practicing member of the California Bar."

I wasn't trying to be funny, and nobody laughed.

10

The only criminal investigator I knew was Emily Winder at the Contra Costa County Public Defender's Office. The next morning, after the kids left for school, I called Emily and asked her how I could find out about a contractor's criminal convictions.

"Easy," she said. "Give me his name and I'll look him up."

"I spelled out Tom's full name and listened to the clicking of Emily Winder's keyboard.

"Two felony convictions," Emily said, "one for fraud, and one for burglary."

Fraud? Burglary? Couldn't be better. "What year?"

"2006 and 2007."

"Great," I said.

Nobody says *great* when learning that the contractor who had free access to her home has recent fraud and burglary convictions—unless the person is preparing for a legal confrontation and wants admissible evidence of moral turpitude. "How can I get more information about the convictions?"

"The convictions were in Santa Cruz. You can drive there yourself, or hire a local investigator to go to the courthouse and pull the records."

"Do you know any investigators down there?"

"Let's see. Just a minute. Okay, here's a name. Brant Willis."

She gave me Brant Willis's number, and the case numbers for Tom's convictions.

I thanked Emily and then called Brant Willis, who answered his phone on the second ring. He said he'd be happy to go to the courthouse and photocopy the documents. He told me his fee, and I said fine.

I called Eric and gave him the news. He said, "I gave a burglar the key to my house. I exposed my family to this guy."

I said. "I'll send this information to Howard."

Later that afternoon Nathan wandered into the kitchen and said, "Mom. What's that drug group you worked for?"

"It is an organization that tries to get laws changed. Why?"

"Is it true that you were trying to legalize drugs like heroin?"

"If you put it that way, it sounds like I believe it's okay to use drugs like heroin. I don't. But the organization believes the criminal drug laws create more problems than they solve, and that jail doesn't help with an addiction. People who use drugs are sick and need help. The organization I worked for wants to see drug users get the help they need."

I was not as naive as I sounded. I knew full well that some kids at the high school and middle school experimented with drugs, and that some, but not all, were sick and in need of help. However, given Nathan's willingness to get up on the school roof because he thought he had a legal defense, I was careful with my explanation.

"Hm," Nathan said.

"Why are you asking?" I asked.

"I'm just curious."

"What made you curious?"

"Nothing."

We were at a dead end. When one of the twins decided not to talk, nothing would get words out of that child's mouth. I felt the way I often felt after a conversation with one of my thirteen-year-olds. The underlying point of the conversation was wholly lost on me.

After Nathan went into his room and shut the door, Jocelyn walked into the kitchen and leaned her elbows on the counter. "Do you want a snack?" I asked.

"Do we have pudding?"

"I'll make some." Somehow I had turned into the quintessential Jewish mother, using food to induce conversation.

I was at the stove, stirring the pudding, and Jocelyn was at the table in the breakfast nook. It was easy to see why the food thing worked. The warm, comforting chocolaty smell might have been what prompted her to say, "I know why Nathan was asking about that drug organization."

Jocelyn heard everything that happened in the apartment. I suspected she knew more about Eric's arrest than she let on. Nathan, on the other hand, heard nothing. How could he from behind closed doors with earphones on his head?

"Why did he ask?"

"There's a guy at school bugging him."

"Oh," I said, even though I couldn't see the connection. "What about this guy?"

"Everyone says he does drugs."

"Ah. Do you think he does?"

"I dunno. Maybe."

"What does Nathan do when the guy bugs him?"

"He tries to ignore him."

"Good," I said. "That's what he should do."

Eric and I told Nathan he should always walk away from fights. During the past six months, on two separate occasions, boys at the middle school had been threatened with knives. Whenever we told Nathan to walk away from a fight, he argued. He said sometimes you can't walk away. I said you don't know whether someone has a gun or a knife, and if the other guy has a weapon, you can't win the fight. Nathan said but if a friend is in trouble, you can't walk away. (Nathan was a pack animal and fiercely loyal to his friends.) Eric said you can help your friend more by going to get help.

I asked Jocelyn, "Do you know why the guy bothers Nathan?"

"No." Jocelyn turned away, which meant she had reached her limit of how much she was willing to say. Jocelyn, reserved by nature, was careful with what she revealed. Something was going on, but I'd have to wait until the kids were ready to talk.

My cell phone rang. I recognized the incoming number as Paula's. I considered not answering, then decided what the heck. "Hello?"

"Why didn't you tell me who you were?" Paula was angry.

"You're such an expert on the contract, I figured you'd actually read it. My name is right there. My name is also on the invoices and canceled checks, which you should have looked at before accusing me of not paying my bills."

Paula absorbed this, and said: "I represent Mullin Construction—"

"Cut the pretentious crap. It's just a sole proprietorship, and a dump. You represent Tom Mullin."

With deliberate calm, Paula said, "I am calling because I have the authority from my client to make an offer. My client is willing to let you walk away without paying anything if you stop accusing him of substandard work."

I forced myself to breathe deeply and count to five. Matching Paula's deliberate calm, I said, "My civil procedure professor gave our class a warning that I'd like to pass on to you. He said, 'Be careful who you represent, because you will become like your clients.'"

"You just don't like that I represent Tom Mullin."

"I just don't like that you sent me a letter full of lies, and then apparently advised your client to do the same. Yes, Virginia, there *is* a code of legal ethics."

"Cassie, the person without ethics is your husband. I'll warn you that you have a few more surprises coming."

I hung up, my hands shaking. *No, Paula*, I wished I'd said: *You and your client have a few surprises coming.*

The printer that worked as a scanner and fax machine was clicking. There was no room anywhere else in the apartment for the printer, so I ran the cords into the closet. I went to look. Coming through the machine were the documents Brant Willis had copied.

I waited for the pages to come through, then sat at the card table in the kitchen and started reading. Turned out, Tom's criminal cases had settled, so there were fewer than fifty pages to copy and fax. The story apparently started when a guy named Anthony Carter advertised a motorcycle for sale. Tom answered the ad, introduced himself as Billy Mason, and arranged with Anthony to test drive the motorcycle. At the time of the test drive, Tom and Anthony agreed that some work needed to be done to get the motorcycle in good shape, and they agreed on a price before the work: $19,500.

Tom wrote a check but asked Anthony not to cash it for three days because that was how long it would take him to deposit the cash. Anthony said fine. Tom said meanwhile, he wanted to work on the motorcycle to fix the problem they had identified. They signed an agreement whereby Tom would work on the motorcycle in Anthony's garage, and if the check didn't clear, Anthony would get to keep the repaired motorcycle without paying. The check Tom wrote was imprinted with Billy Mason's name and an address. Anthony, feeling safe with the check in hand, showed Tom where to find a key to the motorcycle so he could start up the engine while he did the work.

The next day, Anthony came home to find the motorcycle gone. He went to the bank and found out the account had been closed three weeks earlier. He called the police to report the motorcycle stolen. The police, following the contact information on the check, contacted Billy Mason, who said that he'd closed the account when he discovered a box of checks missing from his desk. He was not able to give a complete list of people who'd had access to the house because he lived with four young men who had frequent parties.

The police brought Billy Mason and Anthony Carter face to face. Anthony said, "Nope. That's not the guy."

Tom might have gotten away with the theft if not for the confidential informer who called the police and gave the address where Tom Mullin and the motorcycle could be found. When the police arrived and asked Tom about the motorcycle, Tom produced a sales agreement signed by Anthony Carter.

When first questioned by the police, Tom gave bald-faced lies. He said, "I bought it from a guy named Anthony Carter. I paid cash."

The police arrested him. An investigation showed that Tom had falsified the sales agreement by cutting and pasting Anthony's signature from their other agreement, and then photocopying the documents. Further investigation by a handwriting expert showed that Tom had written the check to Anthony Carter and forged Billy Mason's name. Turned out Tom and Billy Mason knew each other. Billy Mason told the police that Tom had probably been trying to get back at him. He explained that ever since they had both applied for the same firefighter position, which Billy had gotten but Tom had not, Tom had harbored a grudge against Billy.

Tom was charged with three counts of fraud and two counts of theft: One count of fraud was for passing a check he knew to be bad, the second was forging a name on a document, the third was identity theft. The first count of theft was for taking possession of the motorcycle on false pretenses, and the second was for stealing a check from Billy Mason's checkbook. Because he had instructed Anthony to deposit the check after three days, he was also charged with attempted bank fraud. In a plea agreement, Tom pled to one count of felony fraud in exchange for dropping the other charges, and in exchange for a light sentence. Tom served less than a year.

It wasn't the crime of the century, but it showed Tom eas capable of falsifying documents, forgery, and telling a bald-faced lie to a police officer. Because Anthony Carter had believed his entire story, it also showed he could lie convincingly. It was hard to tell whether Tom had devised the fairly elaborate scam before getting started, or whether he had invented as he went along. If Billy Mason was correct in his assessment, the crime also showed Tom to be vindictive.

Tom had come so close to getting away with the theft, you had to wonder what else he had done without getting caught. It was also clear that we'd been wrong about Tom. He wasn't a bumbling and incompetent fool. He was a wily con artist and a practiced liar.

11

Nathan sat at the kitchen table, swinging his leg, kicking the lower cabinet behind him: *bang, bang, bang.*

"Nathan," I said, "I've told you: Don't kick the cabinets."

"I'm not," he said.

I turned, put my hands on my hips, watched him and waited. He said, "I'm not kicking the *cabinets*. I'm only kicking *one* cabinet."

Jocelyn, in the next room, laughed.

I said, "That's not an absolute defense, Nathan. It just means you're not guilty as charged. All I have to do is recharge the crime. Now, stop kicking the *cabinet.*"

"Fine," he said. "You just need to be clear."

"Nathan, sometimes—"

Eric came in from work and called out, "Hello everyone." I sensed from his tone that he hadn't heard anything from Howard—at least he hadn't heard anything bad. Funny how you adjust to things. We'd somehow adjusted to the unsettling fact that Eric was under criminal investigation.

Walking into the kitchen, he said, "I figured we could use some good news," and put some papers on the kitchen table. I'd seen enough contractor invoices the past few weeks to recognize the light weight of the paper and the various colors—yellow, pink, white. "Final invoices," he said, "from the stucco crew, the electricians, and Big Dave. The work is finished."

"We can move back home?" Nathan asked.

"We can start bringing our stuff back tonight," Eric said. "The twins can help."

"That *is* good news," I said.

I selected lemon yellow for the walls in the baby's room and pure white for the trim. Eric painted the room. I like pink, but if you have a girl you can overload on pink the way you can get sick of too much sugar. With brightly colored pictures on the walls and a shelf of stuffed animals, the new room snapped to life.

Being home again made me understand why someone might hand Tom ten thousand dollars to make him disappear. I suspected that if we were willing to give Tom enough money, the criminal charges would disappear as well. How nice it would be if all the troubles disappeared without having to worry about how to win a lawsuit and how to prove that Eric had been framed.

One of my baby care books has a reminder to new mothers: Don't forget to take time to enjoy your baby. With older children and a house under construction, *enjoy your baby* seems like an impossible luxury. So that evening, I put on some quiet music and sat with Rebecca in the rocking chair, calmed by the satiny feel of her cheek against mine.

Now that the project was finished, we could file our complaint with the Arbitration Association. With the help of some do-it-yourself law books, I drafted the complaint. When I finished, the main paragraphs read:

Mr. Mullin breached the contract through his excessive delays, and through his substandard work and code violations. Mr. Mullin ignored city correction notices and kept building in violation of city ordinance and permit requirements. Mr. Mullin poured the foundation in the wrong place resulting in the frame hanging off the foundation 2.5 inches. Mr. Mullin did not shear a wall as required by the plans.

We had to hire a structural engineer to design a solution to the resulting structural defects. We had to hire electricians to correct the numerous code violations and hazards in Mr. Mullin's electric wiring. The plumbing, fascia board, gutters, trim, door jambs, subfloors, and attic and subfloor vents were also of substandard quality and had to be redone.

It was all very matter-of-fact, standard contract dispute stuff. It was fine, and captured the extent of the errors, but it seemed to me there was more. I checked my law school outlines and added:

In addition to substandard work, Mr. Mullin fraudulently concealed errors, including electrical fire hazards. Mr. Mullin fraudulently represented to us that certain inspections had been completed, and collected money from us based on those fraudulent representations. Mr. Mullin induced us to sign the contract by fraudulently representing that he had completed work at another home which in fact, he had not done. Finally, Mr. Mullin violated the contract's implied covenant of good faith and fair dealing.

To say that Tom violated the contract's implied covenant of good faith and fair dealing is your classic understatement, but I figured sometimes it doesn't hurt to state the obvious.

That evening, after reading the full complaint, Eric actually walked around the house whistling. First he whistled the theme songs from the Flintstones, and then the Jetsons. "When Tom sees this," Eric said, "he's going to think: *Uh-oh. I'm in trouble now.* He's going to see that we are not rolling over like his other victims."

"The problem is," I said, "how are we going to collect? He's probably broke."

Eric left the room, and came back fifteen minutes later, whistling again. He handed me a printout from the recorder's website. Evidently, Tom owned a house on the other side of town, in Sutter Park.

"I think we should go for a little drive," Eric said.

"Good idea."

I told the twins we'd be back in twenty minutes and put Rebecca in her car seat. We drove in silence. Sutter Park was in the part of town where the houses were newer and the lots larger. We drove slowly down Tom's street, looking for the house. Turning a corner, we saw a three-story cream-colored house with two large dumpsters in front filled with debris.

"Must be that one," said Eric. "I can tell from the mess."

We stopped across the street. "Yep," I said. "There's his trailer."

The house had a stucco exterior. The façade had Tudor details. Brown trim contrasted nicely with the cream-colored stucco. It had never occurred to me, after seeing Tom's work, that he might have good taste. "His wife probably picked the colors," I said.

The problem with the house was that it dwarfed the other

houses on the block. The other houses were neat and tasteful two or three-bedroom homes. Tom's house was three stories and sprawling. From what I could see around the side, about halfway back the house stopped being charming and took on a more modern look that seemed out of place in that neighborhood.

The garage door was open. Inside tools were strewn on benches and on the ground. There were piles of lumber and rickety sawhorses. Eric said, "This is what he's doing with the money he got from the Snowdens and us. He's paying Paula Armstrong, and working on his house."

"At least he has money for us to collect," I said.

"He sure does."

As we watched, the door in the back of the garage opened and a large-boned, sandy-haired man walked into the garage. "That's him," Eric said, and we drove away, safe in our belief that we had not been seen.

The next day, I emailed Howard to tell him that our litigation with Tom was moving forward. Howard called and said, "Cassie, why don't you come in for a few minutes? I want to talk to you."

"I'll have to bring the baby," I said.

"That's fine."

Howard's office was less than three miles away. Because River Park was close to a freeway entrance, I could get to his office in less than ten minutes. I arrived at his office twenty minutes after we hung up. He invited me into the conference room. I had to talk to him while pacing to keep Rebecca from fussing.

"I'm sorry to tell you this, Cassie, but finding out that your contractor has those convictions doesn't help much."

"How can it not help? He has a history of lying and stealing. He defrauded other homeowners. Our theory is that he framed Eric. Doesn't this make our theory more plausible?"

"Certainly it makes it more plausible. The problem is that the prosecutor said Tom is not the informant."

"He *isn't?*"

"No."

"Who *is?*"

"They're not saying. All Steve will tell me is that the informant absolutely isn't Tom. The fact that workers on the construction site were into meth doesn't mean that Eric isn't also into meth."

"This is ridiculous. I think I'd know if my husband used drugs. I'd have seen some sign of something. He's precise like clockwork."

"Nobody is accusing Eric of *using* meth. They're not even accusing him of selling meth. Turns out, they're accusing him of being what's called a mule. A mule is a middle guy who is completely clean. All he has to do is pick up a package from one place and deliver it to another, and he gets as much as twenty thousand dollars. It's hard to pass up a quick way to earn that kind of money."

"I'd know if we had an extra twenty thousand dollars somewhere. I know all of our accounts, where all the income is from. It's not possible."

"Your husband fits the profile for a mule. He fits the profile exactly. Male, not too young, not too old, clean, never in trouble. Part of the profile is a person with a sudden need for extra cash. A guy whose house is being trashed by a contractor and whose wife just had a baby is a guy who can use some quick cash. The litigation gives Eric a motive for accusing Tom."

What I felt, in that moment, was sick. Once, when the

twins were in preschool, our car had broken down and we'd had no cash in our pockets and needed to get home because the babysitter had to leave, so we'd gotten on the light rail without paying. The penalty for getting caught on the train without a ticket was $25. Eric spent the ride in a state of anxiety afraid he'd be caught. After sixteen years, you know if your husband has it in him to commit a felony.

"You're saying you believe that my husband is guilty."

"I'm saying that the case against him is looking pretty solid. They did the voice analysis, and could not say conclusively that it was his voice. But they couldn't say conclusively that it wasn't his voice, either. It was fifty-fifty, but they're saying the balance leans toward it being his voice."

"Fifty-fifty with a lean one way is not *beyond a reasonable doubt.*"

"When your only defense is that guilt hasn't been established beyond a reasonable doubt, you're in trouble. The evidence is adding up. Someone calls a cell phone number from your house phone one evening at six fifteen, the time your husband is usually at the house. The message says, 'I have the package ready.' The next day, the police watch a guy knock on the door, speak to your husband, enter the house, and come out with a package of methamphetamine."

"I want to know who the informant is."

"They'll never tell us that. They would tell me only that whoever it was cut a deal with the prosecution after being stopped with methamphetamine, and it wasn't Tom."

I sank into a chair, patting Rebecca's back to keep her from fussing. "I guess the informant could have been anyone who worked on our property in the past few months, who knows the project, and cut a deal with the prosecutor."

"Unfortunately the D.A.'s office thinks the evidence

taken together is convincing because they've decided they'll be charging Eric with running methamphetamine. The arraignment will be Monday at 2:00. You'll have to be prepared because the word might get out."

"So none of this helps?" I asked, pointing to Gina and Tom's witness statements and the papers showing Tom's convictions.

"Of course it helps. It helps with our defense. What I'm saying is that they have enough evidence to charge Eric with the crime. Charging him is a win-win strategy for them. They charge Eric, and he either comes forward with better evidence and they drop the charges, or he settles. What do they have to lose?"

"Eric will not settle."

"Then we'll go to trial. Trials get expensive."

"We have equity. We have retirement funds."

"All right, Cassie. But prepare yourself because these things get messy. We'll put our best defense together, and I believe it will be a good one, but there's no predicting what a jury will do."

12

We had agreed to tell the twins as soon as we knew for sure that charges would be filed, but neither of us felt ready so we decided to put off telling them until after Eric was actually charged. Monday was three days away. Anything at all could happen. That evening, after I gave Eric the bad news, he went to the gym to relieve his stress. We acted as if nothing out of the ordinary was about to happen.

Saturday night, after all three children were asleep, Eric poked his head through the doorway and said, "Your phone. I answered it." He handed me my cell phone. "It's Kristin," he said. "Tom's employee."

"The out-of-work travel agent?" I took the phone. "Hello?"

"Hey," said Kristin. "Remember me?"

"Of course. Are you still working for that scum bag?"

"No. What an idiot I was. You sure turned out to be right. So, so right. I've been wanting to tell you that. I'm embarrassed it took me so long to figure out what was going on. How are you guys doing?"

"Not so good. I'm afraid Tom Mullin is torturing us and ruining our lives."

Eric, standing nearby, whispered, "Be careful what you tell her." I nodded to him.

"You and a lot of other people," Kristin said. "Boy do I have stuff to tell you."

"Tell me."

"How about this. The last day on the job, Tom took a stack of orange correction notices from your job and told me and Carrie to shred them. He laughed and said they were bullshit. That was when Carrie knew something was up."

"That's good," I said. "Concealing correction notices from homeowners. Would you be willing to give me a witness statement?" Even if none of this stuff would convince the prosecutor Tom was framing Eric, at least we could make sure to win the civil case and collect the money to pay for a criminal trial.

"I'm happy to give you a witness statement. Carrie will, too."

Instead of asking who Carrie was, I said, "So Carrie knew he shouldn't be concealing correction notices from us?"

"Yup. Her dad's a contractor. At first, she believed Tom and felt sorry for him when he talked about his difficult clients not paying him for work he'd done. She knows from her father that some homeowners can be difficult. But when Tom laughed about the correction notices and shredded them, she knew. I mean, there were other clues before then. That's when she knew he was cheating his customers."

"Who is Carrie?"

"Another of our friends who worked for Tom. Really, the reason I'm calling is to introduce you to Tammy Sherwood, who worked as his bookkeeper for a few months. She's the one with all the information. Here she is."

There was a shuffling and someone said, "Hi, I'm Tammy. I understand Tom filed a lawsuit against you."

"How do you know that?"

"He's suing everyone, or everyone is suing him. So far six of his employees have gone to the labor board because he won't pay them. I can't go yet because he's suing me, and the labor commissioner people told me that I can't file a complaint until my litigation with him is over."

This was an overload of information. To focus on one detail, I asked, "How did you know he was suing us?"

"I saw it on the Superior Court web page. That's when Angie and Carrie thought we should call you."

I didn't know such information was available on the Superior Court web page. I opened my web browser and asked, "Who is Angie?"

"Angie's a notary public. She's the one who notarized all those lien statements, including yours. Just so you know, I'm the one who wrote your final invoice."

"What final invoice?" I asked.

"You never got the final invoice?"

"No. I never got a final invoice."

"Just a minute." To someone in the room with her, she said, "They never got their final invoice." Meanwhile, I found the civil case index on the Superior Court web page where you could enter a name and see what litigation the person was involved with. I typed "Tom Mullin" and up came eleven listings. Eleven! All filed within the past six months.

Tammy said, "Do you want me to fax you the final invoice?"

"Please do." I gave her the number. "I'll call you back after I take a look at it."

While waiting for her to fax the invoice, I clicked on each of the listings on the web page. On each one, Paula Armstrong was representing Tom Mullin. Ours was the fourth listing. In the sixth listing, Tom Mullin was the plaintiff and Tammy Sherwood was the defendant. The case type was "contract dispute / other." Three of the listings were collection agencies suing Tom. One was the labor commissioner versus Tom. One was the Snowdens. The others I didn't recognize.

The fax machine started clicking. The invoice that came through was in spreadsheet form, a list of charges with brief explanations. The total was $28,325.31, the exact amount of damages Tom claimed in his superior court lawsuit.

I went to get Eric. "You have to come see something."

First I showed him that Tom was involved in eleven lawsuits. I clicked through and showed him each listing. Then I showed him the invoice and told him that Tammy, Tom's former bookkeeper, had faxed it.

He pulled a chair next to me and we looked at the invoice together. Some of the charges were just plain puzzling. For example, there was a charge of $2,732 for extra sheetrock work. Wasn't putting up walls part of the contract work? Yes, Tom had done extra sheetrock work each time he'd cut and patched the sheetrock, but did he really think he could charge for his mistakes?

Another annoying charge was $1,100 for the plumbing. Surely he didn't think he could charge for his monstrosity of a plumbing creation, particularly because moving the water valve had been included in the contract price. There was a charge of $1,450 for extra electrical work.

"What extra electrical work?" Eric asked.

"I don't know. Maybe he's charging us $1,450 for blowing up our kitchen light. He probably had to work hard to get such a loud and smelly explosion."

Eric laughed and went back to reading the invoice.

"I have to call Tammy back," I said.

"How do you know she's not setting you up? She used to work for him."

"He's suing her. Look." I pointed to the Superior Court web page.

"If that's really her. Who knows anymore?"

I called Tammy back and said, "I got it."

"Good," she said. "I just need to tell you that those numbers were made up out of thin air. They were pulled right out of a hat."

"How do you know?"

"Because I'm the one who made up the numbers."

I felt a chill.

She said, "I never worked for a contractor before. At first I believed him when he said you and your husband commissioned extra work and then wouldn't pay. Then I read your contract and saw extra work was supposed to be in writing before the work was done."

"Did you point that out to him?"

"Yes. I showed him exactly where the contract said that. He just laughed."

"So how did you come up with these numbers?"

"He gave me a copy of the Contractor's Pricing Guide. He described the work he did. He told me to look it up and figure out what a good charge would be. I kept bringing him drafts, but usually he said the numbers were too low. He told me to figure out how to add more. Sometimes he said I should add twenty percent, or figure out a way to make the price higher. He had a box of receipts, but he had three jobs going at once, plus he was working on his own house, and none of the receipts were marked. Sometimes he took a receipt for things in his house and told me to add it to a client's invoice."

"Are you willing to give me a witness statement?"

"Absolutely. Anything I can do to help."

"So why is he suing you?"

"He's accusing me of stealing all of his records. His problem was that he doesn't have any records. The license board called him to schedule an appointment, I think because you and the Pinettes complained about him. The license board expects him to have records that he doesn't have."

I looked at the list of people in litigation with Tom. The Pinettes were in a contract dispute with him. "Did he ever call the police to report his records stolen?"

"Actually, I did. He called me the night his warehouse was, quote, robbed, unquote. I got there and thought the whole thing was suspicious. By then my friends and I knew he was a liar, but he owed most of us money, and we needed to get paid so some of us kept working."

"Why did you think the burglary was suspicious?"

"The robbers only took his computer. He had a stack of CD's, but the robbers didn't take those. He told me to call the police and report it, so I did. That was Thursday. Friday he wanted me to give him all the files I had. After his computer was quote, stolen, unquote, I had to work at home. Friday night I gave him all the files. Carrie was with me. Then Monday before I could go to work, his lawyer Paula Armstrong called and told me that they were suing me for conversion. She told me the court date and mailed me a document. I have to go to court next Monday."

"What document did she send you?"

"Some court thing," she said. "I'm planning to bring lots of witnesses Monday to tell the judge it's all a pack of lies."

"Do you know Paula Armstrong?"

"I've met her a few times. Don't get me started."

Getting her started was exactly what I wanted to do. "Does she believe the stuff he says?"

"She believes everything. She thinks we're all ganging up

on poor Tom, and that we're all taking advantage of him."

"Let me make sure I understand," I said. "Tom and Paula are accusing you of breaking into his office and stealing his computer? While you were working for him?"

"That's right. They're also saying I stole all of his records."

"Paula really believes that?"

"I really think she does. Tom is saying I did it because I was so mad that he wasn't paying me. It's true I was mad about that. By then he owed me three thousand dollars."

Wouldn't you think Paula would start getting suspicious? First he accused the Snowdens of forging his name and defrauding him of thirty thousand dollars. Now he was accusing his bookkeeper of breaking and entering his office and stealing his computer.

"Why wasn't he paying his workers?" I asked. "In November he took a hundred thousand dollars out of his house."

"That was gone in about a week. He had creditors knocking, and he made that big meth purchase, and he gave Paula a big check."

I registered the fact that he'd made a big meth purchase. "How much did he give Paula?"

"I only know about one check he wrote to her, but I didn't actually see the amount because it came from his personal account. She's doing two appeals for him, and those are expensive. I guess he lost two claims with the labor board, and she's appealing."

I was absorbing this when Tammy said, "It was nice talking to you. I have a few other calls to make before it gets too late. Let me give you my telephone number." I reached for a pen and wrote down her number.

"I'm going to call Gina Snowden," she said. "We'll get together soon so I can swear out a witness statement for you."

13

Eric stood in the hallway of the courthouse, looking as if he were being led to his execution. He was pale and tense, his faced pinched, the worry lines in his forehead deeper than usual. I stood on one side of him, Howard on the other.

"The most humiliating part," Eric said, "is this whole thing is public."

"An arraignment is just a formality," Howard told him.

This entirely failed to comfort Eric.

To me, Eric said, "I don't want you to come in. I don't want you to see me like this."

"I know the truth, Eric. By the time this is over, everyone will know the truth."

Howard turned to Eric and said, "Nothing much is going to happen right now. It's administrative routine. The point of this hearing is for the judge to read the charges against you, but we'll waive the reading of the charges. Then we'll waive time. You're not in custody, so time will work for us. Then we enter a plea of not guilty. That's it."

Eric's face remained gloomy. "Fine."

We went in to the courtroom and sat in the back row. Because of the constant whispering and murmuring, the shuffling of papers and scraping of chairs, it was difficult to hear what was happening when those ahead of Eric approached the judge. But just watching the others, it was easy to see that, indeed, this was a matter of routine. Everyone looked bored, including the judge. A lawyer with long hair slicked back and held in place at the nape of her neck, who I took to be a deputy district attorney, stood at a podium. She appeared to be about eighteen, but I figured she had to be at least twenty-five.

Eric's name was called. He and Howard stood up, walked forward, and stood in front of the judge. Eric's back was ramrod straight.

Watching, I felt a flicker of doubt. What if Eric *had* been tempted to pick up an easy twenty thousand dollars? Was it possible to be married to a man for sixteen years and not really know him?

The young lawyer with the slicked-back hair stood by a second podium. Howard waived the reading of the complaint, waived time, and entered a plea of not guilty. Afterward, the young lawyer handed Howard a thin manila folder, her manner crisp and business like. Then it was someone else's turn: Justice, mass produced.

Once outside, Howard tapped the manila folder and said, "Let's walk over to my office and see what we've got here."

We walked the few blocks to Howard's office in silence. As soon as we were seated at Howard's conference table, we discovered the file contained two pages stapled together. One page was a police report, the other showed the results of the voice analysis. Howard unstapled them and asked his assistant, Lisa, to make us each copies.

The only thing we learned that we didn't already know was there were two confidential informants. According to the police report, two confidential informants, referred to as C.I.s, told the police that Eric was a mule. One C.I. showed the police a cell phone call made at 6:15 p.m. from the house phone in which Eric said, "The package will be ready between 6:00 and 6:30." To test the truth of the C.I.s, information, the police watched one of the C.I.s knock on Eric's door, enter the house, and come out a few minutes later with a baggie of methamphetamine wrapped in a jacket. The police called for a warrant, entered the house, searched, and found another smaller supply of meth.

"There are *two* of them?" Eric muttered. "I can't believe one isn't Tom."

"We need more information," said Howard, reaching for a yellow legal pad. On the table was a mug filled with pens. Howard uncapped one of the pens and said, "This is ridiculous. Let's make a list of questions to send over."

He wrote as he spoke: "We need more information about these C.I.s. How did they come to inform? Why did they inform? We need information about the call from the house phone. What day and time was it made? We need the inconclusive results of that voice analysis. We need the details of how the voice analysis was done so we can hire our own expert. We need copies of the search and arrest warrants. We need the lab results on the drugs."

He paused and looked at us for ideas. I said, "What phone number was the 6:15 call made to?"

"They may not tell us that," said Howard. "They make sure to protect the identities of the C.I.'s."

Eric said, "I wonder if we can get the phone company to send us a list of calls made from our house. Maybe we can figure out who the calls were made to."

"Does your phone bill have that information?" Howard said.

"No," said Eric. "We pay a flat rate for local service, so we don't get an itemization of local calls."

"You might be able to request it," said Howard.

"This whole thing is going to drag on for a long time, won't it?" Eric asked.

"Yes, it will," said Howard. "It will take at least a few weeks before I get more complete discovery. As long as you're not in custody, remember that it's not in our best interests to push this quickly."

"All right," said Eric. "I just don't like being in limbo like this, being falsely accused."

Howard had been a criminal defense attorney for more than thirty years. I'd been told by those who had worked with him that his approach was to be charming and gentlemanly with the prosecutors and tough with his own clients. He often yelled at his clients, telling them they were in deep trouble so they needed to pull themselves together and stop bullshitting him.

But now, Howard sat back in his chair and gave Eric a sympathetic look.

Back at home, I put Rebecca in her crib. Nathan was in his room with his door closed, Jocelyn was in her room with the door open. Eric tapped softly on each of their doors and said, "There's something I need to tell you. Come sit in the living room."

Ordinarily when you call the twins, one or both said, "Hold on! Just a minute," a response that always annoyed Eric.

They must have heard something different in his tone because immediately they emerged from their bedrooms and sat on the couch, watching him. Eric and I sat in the winged-backed chairs.

Eric cleared his throat. "You know that we're in a heated

dispute with our contractor—"

"We know, Dad," said Nathan. "We're suing him. Mom is going to *get* him," he punched his fist into his palm. "She's going to give him the ole Elle Woods fire."

The "old Elle Woods fire," was how he remembered a line from *Legally Blonde*.

"In real life," I said, "these things are not a joke."

Eric looked at me, his eyes mournful and sad. I had the sense he wanted me to tell the twins, so I said, "Here is what's happening. Tom is framing your father for a crime he didn't commit. Right now, unfortunately, the police believe Dad committed a crime. We need to prove he didn't."

Jocelyn said, "But Dad shouldn't have to prove anything. Innocent until proven guilty."

"And," said Nathan, "they have to prove it beyond a reasonable doubt."

Spoken like the children of a recent law school grad.

"Right now, unfortunately," I said, "there's some manufactured evidence against Dad, and the evidence looks bad, so we do need to prove that the evidence is false."

"What's the evidence?" Nathan asked in a very grown-up voice.

Eric told the twins the whole story. When he finished, I explained how the usual presumptions about possession didn't apply because we weren't living at the house, and so many people had access.

"Did Dad tell the police that?" Nathan asked.

Jocelyn shot him a look and said, "You're not supposed to tell the *police* that. You're supposed to tell your lawyer."

My children, the experts on what to do if arrested.

"I told my lawyer," Eric said, "who told the prosecutor. Now we have to wait for more information from the prosecutor's office. Listen. This is important. We're not supposed to talk about this with anyone."

"Like on T.V.," Jocelyn said. "If anyone asks us, we say *no comment.*"

"Exactly," I said.

"Can we say Dad is innocent?" Jocelyn asked.

Eric and I looked at each other. "I suppose so," I said, "but nothing else."

"Can we see the police report?" Nathan asked. "Maybe we can help figure out how to prove Dad's innocent."

"I'll make copies for you," I said. "But I want you to keep them very safe in your rooms because I don't want anyone seeing them."

"Mom," said Jocelyn. "We're not stupid."

Eric leaned forward, cupping his fist into his palm. I knew what he'd say if someone asked him just then how he was feeling. He'd say, "This was the most humiliating moment yet." It seemed to me, though, it wasn't as bad as he'd anticipated. The twins had, after all, seen me through law school. Nathan had read the Daffy Duck criminal procedure flash cards. They knew that accused does not necessarily mean guilty.

14

The house phone rang as I was wiping the kitchen counters after dinner. Eric was putting leftovers into plastic containers.

Jocelyn answered the phone and called out, "Mom, it's for you!"

The caller was Gina Snowden. "Hi, Cassie!" Her voice was breathless and sweet. "We have a surprise for you and Eric. Can you stop by for a few minutes?"

"Is it good news?"

To someone in the background, Gina said, "She wants to know if it's good news."

"Don't get her hopes up too much," said a woman in the background. "Tom Mullin's still alive."

Into the phone, Gina said, "I wish we had good news. But we do have something *fun* for Eric."

I supposed a guy just charged with a felony was entitled to some fun.

I asked her to wait a moment and went to tell Eric. His frown deepened into puzzlement and suspicion. "Maybe after Rebecca falls asleep?" he suggested.

I went back to the phone and said, "We can be there in about an hour, after we get the baby to sleep"

"Great. Come when you can."

All the curtains were drawn at the Snowden's house, but the lights were on—the porch light, the upstairs lights, the living room lights. I rang the doorbell and heard a shuffling inside. The door opened and Gina said, "I'm so glad you're here. Come in!"

She led us down the hallway, through the living room, to the family room. She switched on the lights and about three dozen people crowding the room shouted, "Surprise!"

I was entirely bewildered. It wasn't my birthday. It wasn't Eric's birthday.

The house smelled of brewed coffee and freshly baked cookies. Some people held wine glasses, others held paper cups. Then I saw the banner. Strung across the doorway leading to the kitchen was a banner with red and blue lettering that looked as if it had been painted with children's acrylic paint: THE TOM MULLIN VICTIM'S CLUB.

"Eric is the guest of honor," Gina said.

Afraid to ask why Eric was the guest of honor, I said, "The Tom Mullin Victim's Club?"

"It was Tammy's idea," Gina said. "I thought it was great, like an ex-wives club. We got the other homeowner's name and address from the lien notices at the Sacramento Recorder's Office. Tom's done three big projects, yours, ours, and the Pinettes."

Good Tom joined the conversation and said, "We're taking Neighborhood Watch to a whole new level." He patted the small black spiral notebook and pen in his shirt pocket and said, "Our lawyer wants us to write down the names and phone numbers of anyone who might be able to help us."

"Tammy and her friends have been watching the criminal dockets," said Gina, "because they keep hoping Tom will get arrested for something. They saw Eric's name and figured Tom must have accused him of something he didn't do—"

I looked at Eric, knowing he wouldn't be pleased to be the center of attention this way. He wasn't. He's not exactly a gregarious party type under the best of circumstances. Now he looked like he wanted to crawl into a hole.

Kristin and another woman walked over and said hi. I hadn't remembered Kristin being so large. She was tall and lean, but solid.

"Eric," I said. "Did you ever meet Kristin? She helped Tom do the—" I stopped as an image of Tom's contraption of pipes flashed in my mind.

"Plumbing?" Kristin suggested.

"I guess you could call it plumbing," I said, "using the term loosely."

Kristin introduced the woman with her. "This is Tammy Sherwood, the bookkeeper. You talked to her on the phone. She's the one who wrote that invoice."

"That's me," Tammy said. "Sucker extraordinaire."

Tammy was even taller than Kristin, with a narrower build. Why did it seem like everyone connected with the construction industry was big, even a former bookkeeper who sort of fell into the job? Eric and I were small—I was just over five feet, and Eric was five seven—so compared to us, most people were big. But I didn't remember everyone being so big when Tom was on the job. Funny how memory plays tricks. I guessed I was used to being around smallish Jewish academic types, like my best friend Eliza and her husband. After Eric had gotten his glasses a few years before, he came to look like a rabbi, and I was so slight and waifish I'd never be mistaken for a construction worker.

A few others joined us. Tammy introduced us to Carrie,

the one whose father was a contractor and who knew Tom shouldn't be destroying city correction notices.

The doorbell rang again. Gina excused herself and went to open the door. I heard her say, "Welcome to the Tom-Bashing Party."

"Thanks," the newcomer said, "I guess I'm in the right place."

Quietly to Tammy, I asked, "What do you know about Eric's arrest?"

"Here's what I figure. I figure Tom set Eric up to look like a drug dealer. He told me once that one of his employees said that Eric approached him about buying some meth. That was after I realized that nothing Tom says is true, so I laughed it off."

"Which employee?" Eric asked. "I never talked to his employees."

"One of his workers, he didn't say who," said Tammy. "I didn't ask. Sorry."

"Does he have any employees loyal enough to lie for him?" I asked.

"There must be someone," Tammy said. "But nobody I know. Everyone I know is ready to slit his throat."

"So are they getting divorced?" someone asked Gina.

"Those rumors are false," Gina said. "Kelly and Tom are back together. At least my mother said that her mother said they seem to be back together again. She's back to defending him."

"Cassie! Eric!" Good Tom called from the kitchen. "Do you want some wine?"

"I do, actually," Eric said.

Good Tom looked at me. "No thanks," I said. One of us would have to drive.

Eric went into the kitchen. A woman walked up to me, stuck out her hand, and said, "Hi, I'm Angie."

I had to think back to my conversation with Tammy to remember who she was. "Oh, yes," I said, remembering. "You notarized our lien statement."

"That's me. I feel horribly about that. I probably should have known the documents were false, but back then I still believed him. I also feel badly because I'm the one who brought in my friends to work for him. He kept telling me how much trouble he was having hiring good people, and a bunch of my friends needed work just then. Now it's pretty obvious why he couldn't get anyone decent to work for him."

Angie drifted off to say hello to a friend. Around me, several conversations were going on at once. Tammy was telling Gina Snowden about all the creditors who were after Tom. I joined them and asked, "How is Tom paying Paula?"

"He always pays her first," said a man whose name I didn't know. "Tom sent me a few times to deliver checks to her."

"Big checks?" I asked.

"Huge. Sometimes as much as five thousand dollars."

"Hmm," I said. In the world of legal fees, five thousand dollars was not huge. But he *was* paying her, and he was paying her first.

"Speaking of Paula," Kristin said to me, "there's something you might want to know. When we left your house that last day after we did the plumbing, he called Paula, and said, 'get 'em.'"

"Get 'em?" I asked.

"Yup. That's what he said. He said 'get 'em.'"

"Get 'em?" I repeated. "Like the way you might tell a dog 'sic 'em?'"

"Exactly like an attack dog. Or a hatchet man."

"Paula Armstrong does whatever Tom tells her to do,"

Tammy said. "She doesn't question anything."

"How did Tom come to hire Paula?" I asked.

"He did work for her a few years back," said Tammy. "Some small jobs around her house. They got along."

That story sounded too pat to me. "Did you hear that from her, too?" I asked.

"Oh yes. She said he was so disorganized he didn't even know how much she'd paid him. She said she could have easily taken advantage of him."

If by some miracle Tom had actually done good work for Paula, she might believe that evil homeowners were taking advantage of poor, disorganized Tom.

"I just assumed he found her through an ad," I said, "or her website or something like that."

"Nope. She hired him to do work in her house."

"If he spent a lot of time in her house," I said, "who knows?"

"Do you think Tom Mullin and Paula Armstrong are making whoopee?" asked a woman standing nearby.

"I keep trying to figure out what the heck Paula is doing with him," I said. "She's a cinderblock but I never thought she had this kind of thing in her." To Tammy, who seemed the most knowledgeable, I asked, "Do you think they're making whoopee?"

"I really don't think so." Then, gently, Tammy said, "So, do you want to hear the kinds of things Tom said about you?"

"No," I said. I didn't need to get any angrier. Then I said, "On second thought, tell me."

I expected to hear how emotional I was—a hysterical, pregnant woman. But Tammy surprised me by saying, "He said you're very foxy and clever, always tricking him into doing extra work. Every time he talked about you, he said you were a lawyer and sneaky."

"And you believed him."

"At first. But after a while, I knew better. After a while I could see he was cheating you, not the other way around."

"So," I asked. "Are the meth rumors about him true?"

"Absolutely."

"How do you know?"

"I know," Tammy said in her firm, determined way. "I found some meth in a baggie by the keyboard. I showed it to Kelly. Kelly was very upset. She said he promised her he quit that stuff."

I didn't ask Tammy how she knew it was meth in the baggie. Something about Tammy, perhaps her determination or her knowing savviness, gave me the idea that she had grown up without much money. She seemed smart—sharp, actually. I guessed her to be thirty-five or maybe forty.

"If you want to know how messed up his mind is," Tammy said, "Kelly told me that meth calms him. Can you imagine that?"

"No, I can't," I said, taking her word for the fact that if meth calms a person down, he must have a messed up mind. I looked around and said, "Are the other homeowners here? The Pinettes?"

"That's Bev Pinette, over there," Tammy said, pointing to the couch. Bev was in conversation with Gina. "Bev's husband is in the kitchen. Come on. I'll introduce you to Bev. I don't think she wanted to come, but she seems to be enjoying herself."

We walked over to the couch. Bev was saying, "I had actual flames coming out of one of the sockets. The electrician who came to fix the wiring said he'd never seen such a mess. Actual flames. Can you believe it?"

"I believe it," said Gina, looking up at me and Tammy.

"I believe it, too," I said. "I'm Cassie."

"Hi, Cassie," Bev said. "Nice to meet you. I've heard a lot about you." Bev Pinette was tense and prickly, entirely different from the doe-eyed and sweet Gina Snowden. "I'll tell you this," Bev said, pointing her finger, "I had a bad feeling about Tom from the beginning. Right after I signed the contract, I regretted it."

"You're quicker than I am," I said. "It took me months to realize how bad he was."

"When he was still on the job," Bev said, "the roof looked wrong, so I hired a roofing expert. The roofing expert listed everything wrong with the roof and said it would cost twenty thousand dollars to tear down Tom's mess and do it right."

"Calling a roofing expert while he was still on the job was smart," I said.

"Our attorney sent the roofer's report to Tom's attorney, but so far she hasn't responded. Our attorney made a settlement offer: If Tom takes the lien off our house, we'll let him walk away."

"You'd do that?" I asked. What was it with people, paying Tom to walk away? Were they *trying* to keep him and Paula in business? Not that we could hand Tom that kind of money, even if we wanted to. We'd drained most of our equity to build the room. Our cash was gone because of the repairs, and now with the bail, our credit cards were almost maxed out. Plus we might need money to pay for a trial.

"I'd rather take the loss," Bev said, "than go through the headache of a trial, plus having to shell out all that money in attorney fees that we might never get back."

"Eric would never just let him walk away," I said.

"You should see the scathing letters Paula Armstrong wrote

us," Bev said, "demanding that we pay Tom Mullin the money we supposedly owed him. We don't owe him anything. We paid every single invoice he gave us, even the invoices where he added absurd charges."

"Does she know that?" I asked.

"We sent her copies of the invoices and our canceled checks. She doesn't care. What I don't understand is where he's getting the money to pay her. He's appealing a six hundred dollar labor board judgment. He must be paying thousands of dollars in attorney fees to bring an appeal to try to avoid paying six hundred dollars, which shows you how irrational he is."

"He'll have to run out of money eventually," said Gina, "especially if he's hiring Paula Armstrong to appeal six hundred dollar judgments."

"I don't want him to run out of money yet," I said. "Not until we can collect."

"Have any of you seen his monstrosity of a house?" Bev asked.

"Once," I said, "from the street."

"I see it every day. We live a half mile up the hill. From the outside it looks all right. But inside, from what the neighbors say, it's hideous. I guess it's his idea of showy, but the neighbors say it's tasteless—fake marble, Greek columns, the whole works."

"But he puts quality materials into his house," Tammy said. "He uses junk in his client's houses, but only the best for him."

"Because his wife insists," said Bev. "Kelly is no better than he is. Whenever he had a competent crew working at our house, she'd come and order the crew to her house to work there. She knows he's a con artist and doesn't care. All she cares about is living in a fancy house."

I looked around but didn't see Eric anywhere. Gina, who

must have guessed what I was thinking, said, "Eric went into the kitchen."

I excused myself and went to find Eric. He was standing by himself. "Eric?"

"Let's go outside for a minute," he said.

We went to the front of the house and stood on the porch. He said, "I've been listening to conversations. There's more going on than meets the eye. Not with the Snowdens. They're nice enough. But Tom's former employees are talking about wild parties Tom threw—parties they attended."

Eric could be critical and judgmental. "So?" I asked.

"The C.I.s have to be someone close to Tom. People here were all close to Tom. They worked for him. They partied with him. How do we know the C.I.s are not here, in this room?"

"I guess we don't. They might be here. I'm not sure it's a bad thing if they are. If they're around we have a better chance of figuring out who they are. The Godfather said, 'Keep your friends close and your enemies closer.'"

He gave me a look. "The *Godfather*, Cassie? You're quoting The *Godfather*?"

"Maybe it's helpful advice."

He shook his head. "Some of these people helped Tom cheat us. They might not have realized it, but they did. It just makes me uncomfortable."

"But now they hate him, just like us. Come on. Let's go back in."

Eric wasn't persuaded. When we entered, Gina tapped a fork against a glass to get everyone's attention.

"Attention, everyone!" she said, "This party is not only in honor of Eric, the only member of our club so far to be *officially* accused of something he didn't do, but—" she turned to Eric and said, "we also have gifts for Eric. Everyone here is willing to swear out a witness statement that Tom is a lying, cheating, scumbag, which should help with his criminal defense, and his lawsuit for damages."

She looked to see our reactions. We were surprised.

When the conversations started back up, Eric whispered to me, "There's something absurd about this."

"There's *something* absurd?" I whispered back. "This is beyond absurd. I feel like I've stepped through the looking glass. A guy trashes our house, you're arrested for a felony, and people we don't even know line up to testify for you?"

Kristin walked over and said, "Can I do the first witness statement? I have to get up early in the morning."

"Certainly," I said, sitting down in front of the computer, which was booted up and ready to go. "Let's start at the beginning. How long you've known Tom, how you started working for him, that sort of thing."

I typed as Kristin explained that when the travel agency she was working for went bankrupt, Angie told her about one of her clients, a contractor who seemed really nice, who was having a hard time hiring good people. "At first," she said, "I thought he was a nice, scatterbrained guy. By the time I figured out he was a crook, it was too late. He already owed me six weeks pay so I felt stuck until I could get the money."

One at a time each of Tom's former employees sat at the table across from me and swore out a statement that in his or her personal experience, Tom was a liar and a cheat. A few tossed in examples. One said Tom ran a dummy wire to fool city inspectors. Another said that he used scrap material but billed the client as if he'd used prime materials.

After I'd taken down fourteen witness statements I was feeling a little weary. Rebecca, who rarely slept longer than three hours at a stretch, would probably wake up soon. The twins were okay taking care of her for short periods. I went to find Eric to tell him we should be going. He was standing in the kitchen, talking to Good Tom, holding a mostly empty glass of wine. A few others were in the kitchen.

"Cassie," he said. "Get this. They say Tom is paranoid. They say he has thousands of dollars of video surveillance equipment around his house."

"He's paranoid for real," I asked, "as in psychotic?"

A man with red hair turning gray and thick sideburns said, "He's paranoid for real. He takes videos of everything that happens around his house. He has a picture of Tammy Sherwood driving past, and he's using that to try to prove something against her, I don't get what."

I looked at Eric, remembering the evening we'd driven down his street and sat for a few minutes in front of his house. How embarrassing that would be if he caught us on tape.

"He thinks everyone is out to get him," someone else said. "He's always imagining that people are cheating him."

"And here we all are," I pointed out, "ganging up against him for real."

15

Nathan had already left for school, but Jocelyn was still in her room with the door closed. At 7:30 I called to see how she was doing.

She didn't answer. This should have alerted me to trouble. The bathroom smelled of hairspray. There was going to be a dance after school that day, so I imagined Jocelyn was doing more primping than usual. For the past few weeks, she and Amanda and Kayla had been on the outs. When I asked why, she told me that Kayla and Amanda had spread false rumors about her. As of yesterday, however, the ruptured friendships seemed to be repaired. All three girls had gone to the shopping mall.

Jocelyn came out of her room. When she opened her door out came the sickeningly sweet smell of perfume. Her hair, touched up again so it was deep Pulse Red, was sticking out in a new spiky style. The spiky hair I could live with. The problem was that she was also wearing a short-short denim miniskirt with black lacy trim, and high-heeled sandals. I had never seen the skirt or the shoes before.

"No," I said. I'd gone along with the Pulse Red hair, and I'd ignored the heavy black eyeliner. This was where I put my foot down. "You are not going to school in those clothes. Go right back into your room and change."

Jocelyn glared at me. It was going to be a showdown. "My friends said this looks good on me."

Presumably the friends were Amanda and Kayla. "I don't care. You are not wearing high heels with a short skirt."

"I don't have any other shoes to wear with this skirt," Jocelyn said, as if that were any sort of reason for a thirteen-year-old girl to walk out of the house looking exactly like a tramp.

"You're not wearing that. Besides," I said, aware that I was steering toward irrelevancy, "it's cold outside."

"I'm not cold." Jocelyn stood with her hands clenched into fists and her arms crossed over her chest. "I don't have time to change."

I had the feeling I was reenacting the argument of the ages. Knowing you're living an archetypal moment, however, does not lessen the distress.

"Because you are so young," I said, "you don't know what kinds of signals you give going out dressed like that. People might think you want to look trampy."

Jocelyn's face reddened and her eyes glazed with tears. "You called me a tramp!"

"Don't twist my words. I did not."

"Yes, you did! You said I'm a tramp!"

"Looking like a tramp is different from *being* a tramp."

Nathan would have argued. Jocelyn preferred theatrics. She turned and ran into her room and climbed the ladder to her loft bed. Having a ladder interfered with her dramatics because she couldn't just run into her room and fling herself across her bed sobbing. She had to climb a ladder, sobbing, which doesn't have the same effect.

I went into the living room to let her cry it out, and to wait for her to change clothes.

She didn't emerge until five minutes after eight. She was wearing jeans and a skimpy tee-shirt and the high-heeled sandals. I wanted to make her change her shoes as well, but the truth was that I'd seen other girls at the middle school dressed in jeans and high-heeled sandals. I decided to let it go.

Jocelyn stood and stared at me, expecting me to challenge this outfit as well. When I didn't say anything, she said, "I'm late for school."

"Yes, you are," I said.

"I need a note for being tardy."

"Not until you admit that I didn't call you a tramp."

She glared at me. "You split hairs like a lawyer and you argue unfair!"

I was shocked. I folded my arms across my chest. "If you want the note, you'll admit I didn't call you a tramp."

"Fine," Jocelyn said. "You didn't say I'm *really* a tramp."

I went to write the note.

I received the documents from the Arbitration Association shortly after Rebecca settled down for her morning nap. I printed out Tom Mullin's three-paragraph answer to our claim and his counterclaim. Reading it made me as deeply angry as if Tom were back in our house blowing up lights and cutting the sheetrock. I had to pace up and down the hallway and take deep breaths before I could go back and read it more carefully:

> *On December 30, 2008, plaintiffs told Tom Mullin to pack up his tools and leave the job site. In compliance with their request, he packed his tools and left. Plaintiffs refused to allow him back again. On December 30, 2008, the project was progressing toward completion. On December*

30, 2008, all city inspections had been done and approved. All of the work done as of that date was in full compliance with building codes and regulations. Mr. Mullin's plumbing work was up to code. Any code violations in the electrical work were the fault of Mr. Sanders, and not Mr. Mullin.

As of December 30, 2008, plaintiffs were behind on their payments to Mullin. Specifically, plaintiffs owed $13,135 for work performed under the contract, and for additional work performed at plaintiff's request.

Mr. Sanders breached the implied covenant of good faith and fair dealing by soliciting Tom's employees to buy methamphetamine from him and then taking revenge on Tom when they refused.

Rebecca was in a deep sleep. Gingerly, I picked her up, wrapped her in heavy blankets, and laid her down in the stroller and put up the top for extra warmth. What I needed just then, to calm myself down, was some fresh air and exercise. Living in California means being able to go for walks all year. I went as far as the zoo, then went the other way as far as Freeport Boulevard. No matter how tense I feel, a brisk walk through River Park calms me. The neighborhood is lovely—the quiet streets lined with English elms, the homes all built in the 1920s and 1930s, the architectural styles including Tudor, Spanish, colonial, high-water bungalow, and cottages.

I arrived back home an hour later and put Rebecca back into her crib. I called Eric and, bracing myself for his reaction, read the answer and counterclaim to him.

"That son of a bitch," he said. "I want to know the name of the employee who's saying that about me."

"We're not going to know until three days before the hearing." I'd read the arbitration rules.

"Every single sentence she wrote is a lie," he said. "Which inspections were done was a matter of public record."

"I know. The arbitrator should know that, too."

"How dare they blame *me* for the electrical code violations? We're going to get him back, Cassie. He's not going to get away with doing this to us."

I didn't hear Jocelyn come into the house. At four thirty, I noticed her bedroom door closed. Dances usually didn't end until closer to six. I knocked on Jocelyn's door and opened it softly. She poked her head over the edge of the loft bed. She had tears on her cheeks and her eyeliner was smeared.

"Why aren't you at the dance?"

"I'm just not."

Guilt made me wonder if she wasn't at the dance because she was in jeans instead of a miniskirt. I climbed up the ladder and sat on her bed.

"Were Kayla and Amanda mean again?" I asked.

Jocelyn looked away. From her silence, I knew I'd guessed right.

"What did they do?"

She was still looking away toward the wall. "It was just Kayla."

She had evidently forgotten our quarrel that morning. A middle school day is so long, particularly when you're in tears at the end of it, the quarrel over clothes probably seemed a century ago. "What did Kayla do?"

"I was going to the dance with Ryan. Yesterday Kayla teased me about why I would want to go with him. Then at lunch today, she asked Ryan if he would go with her instead."

"And he went with her." I made it a statement instead of a question so she wouldn't have to respond. She put her head down on her arms.

"Sweetie," I said. What else can you say at a moment like that? I couldn't tell her again what I really thought of Kayla any more than you bad-mouth a friend's husband after they've quarreled. I had already told Jocelyn once that I didn't think Kayla was really her friend. There was nothing more to do.

I wanted to say something sympathetic, without specifically trashing Kayla. What I came up with was: "I don't like anyone who is mean to you."

"Then there are a lot of people you don't like," Jocelyn said gloomily.

Rebecca was wailing at the top of her lungs. I paced the hallway with her on my shoulder, singing *Twinkle, Twinkle Little Star*, trying to soothe her. Jocelyn believed that *Twinkle, Twinkle, Little Star* was Rebecca's favorite song, and that she stopped crying when she heard it.

My cell phone rang. Eric was calling again.

"Jocelyn, sweetheart, can you take Rebecca for a minute?"

Jocelyn came out of her room and gently took Rebecca from my arms. "You just don't sing it right, Mom."

"All right, you try."

I went into the living room, away from Rebecca's wailing. Eric said, "Are you all right?"

"No. I don't think we can do this hearing ourselves. Paula has been practicing law for ten years. I think they have something up their sleeves. They are not stupid enough to waltz into a hearing with nothing except a pack of lies. All I have to do is think about Paula and I want to scream at her. How am I going to sit in a hearing with her and not reach over and slap her face?"

"Well, then," he said. "The solution is simple. We have to

hire a lawyer."

I was about to say, "With what money?" but I stopped. He knew the problem as well as I did.

In fact, he said, "We'll figure out how to pay for it."

The sudden silence in the house startled me. I went to look. Jocelyn was rocking Rebecca in the rocking chair. I gave her the thumbs up.

"All right," I said to Eric. "I'll call someone."

I knew just who I wanted to call. I found Melissa Garner's work number on the State Bar web page. Melissa had been a year ahead of me in law school, and had taken a job in a law firm that represented homeowners in disputes against contractors. The fact that Melissa, who had earned top grades at Berkeley, had taken a job with this particular firm was enough to convince me that the firm was tops in the state. The only less than perfect part was that the firm was based in San Mateo, a town just south of San Francisco.

When Melissa came to the phone, I said, "Hi, it's Cassie Eisen. Sorry to take you by surprise, but I need a lawyer. I want to hire you."

"Seriously?"

"We have a contractor nightmare. You should see how this guy trashed our house. Plus he's crazy. Plus he's got an unreasonable lawyer. And there's more. I can't do it myself."

I gave her the ten-minute version of the story, including the fact that the contract had a binding arbitration clause with the American Arbitration Association.

"I'll talk to the partner in charge of my office," Melissa said. She had a quiet, serene way of talking that I found comforting. "I'll call you back soon."

My civil procedure professor's theory about clients hiring

attorneys who are like them was not accurate in the case of me selecting Melissa. She was the picture of tranquility. She was what I wanted to be, but wasn't. Melissa and I had met in moot court, where I had taken honorable mention, and Melissa had won first prize. Melissa's real strength was in negotiations. She always came out ahead in a negotiation. She did this while being completely forthcoming and above board. She was just so sensible that she made the other side want to settle with her. I figured if anyone could convince Paula to be reasonable, Melissa could.

Melissa called back and said, "The partner here said we can't take a case this small on contingency. But he's considering another possibility. Can you send me whatever you have?"

"Sure," I said. I sent everything, the structural engineer's report and invoice, the city inspector's notices, a few of the better witness statements, copies of Tom's convictions.

She called again and said, "Donald says this looks like a slam dunk. He also said if we're efficient, we should be able to do an entire hearing with the Arbitration Association in two days. So here's his deal. He's going to give me three days, one day to prepare, and two days in the hearing. Because you're doing most of the work yourself, I can do the hearing for a flat fee of $1,000. You pay the arbitration costs upfront. You don't have to pay us until you collect. If we don't win or you never collect, there's no charge."

The deal sounded too good to be true. "Are you *serious?*"

"I've never done a real hearing or a trial, just moot court stuff. Donald figures I'll come back after three days with a line on my resume saying I've handled my first hearing and won, and I'll be more valuable to the firm."

The part that worried me was that they were sure it was a

slam dunk.

"There's one thing I haven't told you, but I'd rather tell you in person. Actually, a few things. It may not be as easy as it looks."

"How hard can this be? Donald said in thirty years he's never seen such compelling evidence of incompetence and errors."

"How about if I come to your office tomorrow?" I figured it would be harder to change her mind with me right there in her office, sitting in front of her. San Mateo was a two hour drive from Sacramento. I could arrange daycare for Rebecca.

"All right," she said. "We should meet anyway. Bring the photographs and videotape and everything else you have."

Melissa's office was in a modern office building just off the freeway in San Mateo with a spacious lobby housing a museum of local history. Her office was on the sixteenth floor with a view of low buildings. A receptionist sat behind a desk paneled with a deeply polished golden-hued wood. There were fresh cut flowers in a crystal vase on the reception desk. The office smelled of fresh coffee and lemon polish.

The receptionist buzzed Melissa for me. Melissa poked her head around the corner, waved, and led me to her office—a small enclosure with a window facing the corridor. Because of the window, anyone walking by could see what she was doing—a not very subtle strategy for keeping the young associates working. Sixty hour work weeks in these kinds of firms were the norm.

I put the manila folder containing the police report and Eric's criminal complaint on her desk. I told her the whole story, concluding with, "I don't believe Eric is going to get convicted. The house was wide open with people in and out, so the usual presumptions don't apply. But there was evidence to arrest him, so they did."

She looked at me for a few moments in silence.

"They're not playing fair, Melissa."

"I'd say that's an understatement," she said. "His tactics are all here," she tapped the file she'd already started on our case. "He tricked you into signing a contract by showing you a sample of work that wasn't his. After he botched the job, he's claiming you fired him."

"He obviously has someone willing to lie because Tom isn't one of the confidential informants."

"The criminal allegation is embarrassing for Eric, but I'm not sure it's going to make a difference to an arbitrator. I can ask Donald, but it seems to me it isn't a problem. There hasn't even been a preliminary hearing much less a conviction. Eric's defense is that he's been framed by someone connected with the construction. The arbitrator isn't going to want to hear about an arrest if there's been no conviction. He will want to know the facts about the construction."

"They'll try to discredit Eric, though."

"So? We'll discredit Tom, and we have a lot more. We have a stack of witness declarations swearing that Tom is dishonest, and we have evidence of two felony convictions for burglary and fraud. *Fraud*, for goodness sake."

What I felt was relief.

"What else?" Melissa asked.

I told her everything else I could think of, including my own history with Paula.

"I'll call Paula," she said, "and tell her that I'll be representing you at the hearing, so all communication will come to me."

16

Before heading back to Sacramento, I called Eliza to see if she had time to meet for coffee. She did, so we met at a coffee shop in northeast Oakland not too far from the college where she taught. The coffee shop décor was charming: wood beam ceilings, framed art on the walls, homey easy chairs, the comforting smells of freshly baked bread, warm chocolate, and coffee.

Eliza was fun to talk to partly because she radiated empathy. I asked her once, back when we were in college, how she always knew the right thing to say to comfort someone and she said, "Because I've needed comfort so many times myself." She had a way of leaning forward when listening as if trying to take in everything. Her glasses, large and round, gave her the appearance of an owl. She gathered information and ideas the way she collected things. She didn't have one poodle, she had four. She didn't have one book on the English Renaissance, she had an entire shelf. In her living room were stacks of newspaper articles and photographs. Her home was a collection of funky modern art.

Howard said not to talk about the arrest. Telling my lawyer was different, of course. Surely my best friend of twenty years was also different. So over coffee I told her the entire story.

She sat back and adjusted her glasses. "Do you think Paula has something to do with Eric's arrest?"

"Probably. Wouldn't you think so?"

Eliza tapped her fingers on the table, deep in thought, and said, "Do you think Paula is in partnership with this Tom character, or do you think he's fooled her?"

"His former employees think she's fooled, that she believes everything he says. But I can't believe she's that dumb. Nobody can possibly believe all his stories and allegations. No matter what evidence people send her—structural engineering reports, city inspection notices, canceled checks, she ignores it and bulldozes ahead. I believed him at first, but after a while he started to seem fishy. Eric thinks she's willingly and knowingly choosing a life of crime."

"Paula did always want the trappings of success," Elisa said. "And she didn't care how she got it. Do you think I should try to call her and talk to her?"

"I don't think that would be a good idea. And don't forget that you can't say anything at all about the criminal investigation."

"So what is this guy Tom like?"

"I know what you're thinking," I said. "I wondered the same thing. It's possible. He's not bad looking. At first you think he has a friendly, easy smile. Then you get the feeling something's not quite right. Then you start to think he's downright evil."

"Remember how at ease Paula was when she had those two boyfriends? It would be like Paula to get mixed up with this guy, and then not see anything wrong with her behavior."

For a while Paula in college was dating her teaching assistant, the graduate student assigned to grade papers in one of her classes. When he complained that Paula was putting on weight, she took a second boyfriend—this time a visiting professor in one of the laboratories—who didn't think she was at all overweight. Sometimes both her boyfriends visited at the same time, a situation that made everyone uncomfortable except Paula.

"Tom is married," I said.

"Do you think that would stop Paula?"

"I guess not."

"What's Tom's wife like?" Eliza asked.

"They're kind of an odd couple. He comes across like a preppie football jock. She's small and quiet."

We were off the subject of Eric's arrest. This was fine with me. I told her what I knew about Kelly, then we talked about the twins, and Rebecca, and Eliza's teenage daughter.

My cell phone rang. I knew from the incoming number that it was Melissa. I flipped open my phone and said, "Hello?"

"I talked to Paula and introduced myself," Melissa said.

"What did you think? Could you tell from talking to her that she's a barracuda?"

"Believe it or not, she came across as very sweet."

"Trust me on this," I said. "She is not sweet."

"There *is* something I can't figure out."

"Yup," I said. "It's starting. That's what it's like dealing with Paula. There's always something you can't figure out. What is it this time?"

"She said they're having trouble coming up with the fees for arbitration. She tried to talk me into taking this to regular court, which didn't require $2,000 up front."

"But then it will drag out for years and cost him even more in lawyer fees and everything else," I said.

"I know. It didn't make sense."

"How's he paying *her* if he doesn't have the money for the arbitration fee?"

"I really couldn't ask that. But I told her that we are not going to regular court, and we're not agreeing to a delay. We want the hearing as soon as possible."

I knew from the Arbitration rules that if Tom couldn't— or wouldn't—pay his share of the fee, he could still show up and defend himself, but he would not be entitled to bring any counterclaims against us.

"What did she say?" I asked.

"She said they'll figure out how to get the money."

"I hope you'll forgive me," I said, "if I just don't feel sorry for either of them right now."

Back home in Sacramento, I booted up my computer, opened an online legal database, and ran an asset check for Paula Armstrong. Turned out, she owned a house over in William Park, on the other side of Main Street, about two miles from our house. It wasn't far, but was a modest area where the homes were a little run down, the lawns a little less manicured.

That evening, after Rebecca was asleep, I showed Eric the title report. He said, "William Park? She probably owns a mansion over there. Maybe we should go for a little drive."

I told the twins we'd be back in a few minutes. Eric knew the way to Paula's street because it wasn't far from the field where the twins used to play soccer. Her house, located at the end of the block, was easy to find, even in the darkness.

"That's it?" I said, disappointed. A streetlight directly in front illuminated a single-story wood frame house, not large, perhaps two or maybe three bedrooms, with the kind of aluminum windows popular in tract houses from the sixties, and a porch and shingle roof in need of repairs. It wasn't exactly shabby, but it was definitely not where you expected to find a high-rolling civil litigator.

"It's not much," I said, "considering she's been practicing law for ten years."

I imagined scenarios to account for such a modest home: She could have lost money in a divorce, or she could be choosing to live in a modest house and spend her money on travel.

"Here's my prediction," Eric said. "He'll end up suing her for malpractice. When he loses his cases, he'll blame her. You know how he's always blaming people."

I considered this. Then I wondered if Paula was afraid of him, if she'd innocently gotten involved and didn't know how to get out. Then I thought that with such a modest house, maybe she had been dazzled by a contractor successful enough to own a mansion in Sutter Park. She'd boasted that she represented Mullin Construction. Maybe she felt that representing a business was a sign of success. Then I considered the futility and absurdity of trying to analyze Paula and Tom's client-lawyer relationship from the appearances of their houses.

I spun a new fantasy: Whatever work Tom had done in Paula's house suddenly came apart. I imagined Paula coming home one day to find, say, the front porch collapsed or a rush of water as her pipes came loose. She'd call Tom and he'd tell her that it wasn't his fault. Could he help it if there was gravity? Was he responsible for the laws of physics? If her front porch collapsed, maybe she'd understand how we felt.

17

Nathan and Jocelyn came home from school at the same time—an unusual occurrence. From the dining room window, I watched as they came up the walk, both serious and somber.

I opened the front door to greet them.

"Hey, Mom," said Nathan.

"What's wrong?" I asked. They usually hated it when I asked that question because usually they didn't want to tell me.

"We've got a problem," said Nathan.

Nathan sat at the dining room table in his usual chair, and Jocelyn sat in the extra chair pushed into the corner. Nathan said, "Someone stole my house key."

"Do you know who?"

"Yes," said Nathan. "But I can't tell the principal."

"All right," I said. I could understand that. Going to the principal on another student was social and political suicide, not to mention, in certain circumstances, downright dangerous if someone got angry enough for revenge.

"Dad might say I have to," said Nathan.

Eric had a strong sense of what was right or wrong, but that didn't mean he couldn't be made to understand why certain things could not be done. "You don't have to. Tell me about the guy who stole your key."

"He's just a guy," said Nathan.

"Is he mad at you for something?"

"He always seems mad at me for something."

I assumed that this was the same guy who Jocelyn said picked on him, the guy who the kids suspected used drugs.

"How did he steal it?"

"I had it clipped here, to my pocket. He grabbed and pulled and tore my pocket. Then he ran off and laughed."

He showed me his ripped pocket.

"I guess we'll have to get the locks changed," I said. To make Nathan and Jocelyn feel better about this solution, I said, "I've wanted to change the locks, anyway, and make them all the same. I always worry Tom could still get in somehow."

"Thanks, Mom," said Nathan.

"I'll call the locksmith now. If you find yourself in a conversation with that guy, you can tell him he got the wrong key and it doesn't open any of our doors."

"I don't think I'm going to get into a conversation with him," said Nathan seriously.

"I was joking."

Nathan's somber expression didn't change.

"Nathan," I said, "If someone looks like they're going to lose their temper, please just walk away. You never know what can happen in a fight."

Instead of arguing the way he usually did, he gave an exasperated: "I know, Mom."

Didn't I have enough to worry about without a kid mad at Nathan? I had the locks changed that afternoon.

Melissa and Paula agreed on an arbitrator from the list sent by the Arbitration Association, Mr. Day, who had a degree in architecture from Stanford and held general contracting licenses in California, Oregon, Washington, Nevada, and Hawaii. Eric read his resume and agreed that he'd be perfect. "He'll know what a hold-down is," Eric said. "And he'll know they're not supposed to be bent." We picked the date, March fifteenth. The Arbitration Association rented us a room in the local courthouse.

On the Monday before the hearing, with Rebecca was at the daycare center, I spent a full day preparing binders with our evidence and witness list for the exchange scheduled for 5:00 that afternoon. I made four copies of everything, and put together four binders, one for the arbitrator, one for Paula and Tom, one for Melissa and one for us. I'd tabbed and indexed all our evidence in white laminated binders.

If the arbitrator was willing to take sworn declarations instead of live testimony, our only actual witness—other than Eric and I—would be Bill Hayes, the city inspector.

At 4:30 I dropped off a binder at the Association's Sacramento office. At the same time, Eric was across town taking Paula's binder to her office.

I was walking back to my car when Eric called on my cell phone. "I got their evidence," he said, "just a thin manila envelope, can't be more than five or six sheets of paper. And a videotape."

"Did you see her?"

"No. There was a receptionist on her floor."

"What's her office like?"

"It looks like about six or seven solo practitioners share a receptionist. Not very fancy."

We met at the Kingsbury Coffee Shop near the drop-off daycare center. The twins were home. They were supposed to be doing their homework. Jocelyn would be hard at work. There was no telling about Nathan.

I was so eager to see what evidence they had, I sat at a booth without ordering and reached for the envelope. Inside were five documents: A copy of the final invoice Tammy had written, a computer-generated list of the times Tom had called for city inspections, and computer printout of the Superior Court docket showing that Eric had been arrested on charges of possessing methamphetamine.

Eric saw the court docket printout and said, "That son of a bitch."

The last sheet was the witness list with three names: Tom Mullin, Kelly Anders, and Donnell Mayer.

Donnell Mayer? Eric and I looked at each other. I could tell from Eric's blank expression, that Eric had never heard of him, either.

According to the list, Kelly would testify that we refused to make our final payment, Tom would testify that we continually changed the plans and made unreasonable demands on him, and Donnell Mayer would testify that Eric had asked him if he wanted to be cut in on a good meth deal.

"There's no phone number for Donnell Mayer," I said. "They were supposed to give a phone number."

"They have to tell us," Eric said. "Those are the rules."

I called Melissa and asked her to tell Paula we needed Donnell Mayer's contact information. She said no problem, she'd call Paula right away.

Eric was ready to head home and start the search for Donnell Mayer, but I wanted to sit a few minutes to absorb the fact that this was all the evidence they had. "It's weird," I said. "Is Donnell Mayer what they have up their sleeves? There's nothing else here!"

"Donnell Mayer must be their ace."

"What's this supposed to prove?" I said, pointing to the

computer printout of times Tom called for inspections.

Eric took the sheet from my hand and looked at it. "It proves that Tom called for inspections. It doesn't prove the inspections were done or approved. Look, this shows he called four times for an electrical inspection, and on the fourth time he was fined for calling for inspections when he wasn't ready. So it proves he's an idiot."

"Why is Paula submitting this as evidence? Is she going to walk in with a straight face and tell the arbitrator that this printout proves the inspections were done and approved?"

"What's really embarrassing," said Eric, "is that he is this stupid and I can't figure out how to prove he framed me."

We were on our way home when Melissa called on my cell phone. "Paula just returned my call. She's very upset."

"She saw our binder?"

"She didn't say anything about the binder. I guess she was at a function in Berkeley. Someone named Kimberly Steele told her that the word is going around that she is helping a contractor steal from people—"

"Oh, dear," I said.

"Do you know someone named Kimberly Steele?"

"Of course I know Kimberly." Kimberly was another one of our friends from college. "She and Eliza talk all the time. It just figures Kimberly would run and tell Paula."

"I can't describe how angry Paula was—"

"I can imagine. But come on. Paula must have some inkling by now what he's up to."

"Maybe she doesn't. Donald says she can take her client's word for everything, unless it's obvious he's lying."

"How much more obvious does it have to get?"

"I guess she doesn't see it yet, or she's stubborn. Oh, well.

Let her be mad. She can't really expect to win any popularity contests, bringing all these lawsuits against people in her own neighborhood, and against her former classmate."

"Exactly. She should at least expect people to hate her. Did you tell her we need Donnell Mayer's contact information?"

"She said she doesn't have it. I told her the rules require her to give that information before she can call him as a witness and she said she'll try to find it."

I wondered if this was part of their strategy, so that we couldn't talk to Donnell and prepare.

"Did you get their discovery?" Melissa asked.

"They don't have much. I'll send it to you when I get back. There's a DVD. We'll watch it when we get home."

Melissa said, "So you and Eric will be here Wednesday morning?"

"We'll be there," I assured her. Eric had taken off Wednesday to prepare for the hearing, and of course, he'd taken off Thursday and Friday for the hearing.

Once at home, I called out, "Jocelyn! Nathan! Time for a defense team meeting."

They came out of their rooms. "You got something, Mom?" Nathan asked.

"We've got our first real clue. We've got the name of the guy willing to testify against Dad. Donnell Mayer. Now we need to find him."

"Why?"

"Because we don't trust what either Paula or Tom say. We want to talk to him ourselves. How good are you two at Internet searches."

"We're better than you are, Mom," Jocelyn said. "How do you spell his name?"

Nathan might be the one drawn to legal questions, but Jocelyn was the one who'd gone through a detective phase when she was ten, spending one month worth of allowance and all her birthday money on a subscription for a children's detective magazine that came each month with a kit of detective tools—lock pick, magnifying glass, code wheels, fingerprint powder, file cards and special agent I.D. cards.

I showed them the witness statement we'd gotten from Paula. "It's an unusual name," I said, "which should be a heck of a lot easier than sifting through all the John Smiths."

Eric hooked up a laptop for the twins in the living room with Internet access. They were clicking away on the keyboard when Eric took out the DVD and said to me, "Let's see what's on this." We went to the living room and Eric popped it into the DVD player and turned it on. The recording had the static of a low grade home-made movie. The camera was facing the street as our car drove up and parked to the side of the street.

"What the heck?" Eric said.

"That's Tom's street!" His video surveillance cameras must have caught us the day we checked out his house. "Start it over!"

Eric pushed a button to start the DVD over. I started the timer on my cell phone. Turned out we sat in the car across the street from his house for just under thirty-five seconds. I would have thought we sat there much longer, two or three full minutes at least, which just goes to show how the memory plays tricks.

"What's this supposed to prove?" Eric asked. "That he's paranoid delusional and has video surveillance cameras?"

"I think it's supposed to prove that we're crazy and we were stalking him."

"Last I heard," Eric said, taking the DVD from the

machine, "driving on a public street and stopping for thirty-five seconds isn't against any law."

"I'll call Tammy," I said. "Maybe she knows Donnell Mayer."

I dug my cell phone out of my purse. Tammy answered on the second ring. "Hey, Cassie. What's up?"

"We have the name of the guy who will testify against Eric. Donnell Mayer. Do you know him?"

"Donnell. Yes. He's the one with the long pony-tail."

"Oh. I remember him! He was always here. He was here even after everyone else quit."

"He hung out with Jeff, the tree service guy. Do you know Jeff? He has a blond beard."

"Yes," I said. How could I forget the Tree Guy?

"Last I heard," Tammy said, "Donnell was homeless and living in Jeff's backyard."

"That explains why Paula didn't have his contact information. I guess we have to find Jeff. Do you remember Jeff's last name." The very idea of confronting the Tree Guy made me suddenly very tired.

"I do remember the logo of his tree service—a tree with a rainbow over it. I'll call Kristin or Angie or someone else to see if they remember."

I hung up and told Eric that I badly needed a nap.

I woke up an hour later to learn that the twins came up with nothing. This wasn't surprising if Donnell was homeless. This was the second time we'd reached a dead-end. The first time was when we'd tried to get an itemized list of local calls made from our house phone, and the phone company told us that because we paid a flat rate, they did not keep records of the calls.

By the end of the second day, I'd talked to every person who had given me a witness statement, trying to find someone who knew how we could reach Donnell Mayer. Most people remembered Donnell, some remembered Jeff, but nobody knew how to find either of them.

I hadn't found Donnell, but during the hours I spent on the phone, I learned how everyone's litigation with Tom was progressing. The employees were all going one by one to the labor board and testifying for each other. Tom had to go it alone because the labor board would not allow him to be represented by a lawyer.

The Snowden's lawyer was advising them to settle with Tom and Paula. They didn't have a signed contract, a permit, any city inspections, or any documentation of damages because Gina's brother-in-law had finished the project. The Pinettes, who stood to lose more money than us, were also heading for litigation. They also had a binding arbitration clause, and Paula was also trying to convince them to go to regular court, but they wanted to keep their attorney fees low.

By the time we went to bed Tuesday night, I had all the news and gossip, but no clue how to find Donnell Mayer.

18

"I think we're about finished," Melissa said. "If I have any more questions, I can call you."

The three of us—Melissa, me and Eric—had been in her office since ten, going over the evidence and creating an accurate timeline so she'd know how to draw out our testimony. Lunch was veggie sandwiches. We ate while working. We were packing up when Eric's cell phone vibrated. He checked the incoming number and said, "It's Howard."

Melissa and I listened to Eric's side of the conversation: "Yes . . .okay . . . we're in San Mateo. . .if we leave now, we should get there in two hours . . .three copies would be great."

He hung up and said, "He has more discovery."

Once Eric pulled onto the freeway, I put Frank Sinatra on the CD player. There's just nothing like Frank Sinatra for soothing the nerves. Neither of us talked much driving back. Worn out from two days of trying to find Donnell Mayer and all those hours preparing for the hearing, there was nothing much to do now except clear my mind with *Anything Goes, The Best is Yet to Come*, and *Luck Be A Lady*. After the CD played through twice, I closed my eyes and drifted to sleep, opening them again as we approached Sacramento.

There were no parking places near Howard's office, so Eric dropped me off in front and circled the block while I went inside to get the information. Lisa handed me the manila file, thicker than the last one but still fairly thin, perhaps fifteen or twenty sheets of paper.

"This is what we've got so far," Lisa said. "We should get more in the next week or so. None of it has been transcribed yet, but we figured you'd want to see it as soon as possible."

"Thanks," I said. "We do."

Back in the car, I flipped through the file, which consisted mostly of handwritten police reports. "Start reading," Eric said as he swung into traffic.

"C.I.s were arrested for methamphetamine," I read aloud, "and agreed to a deal with the prosecution by giving the name of their suppliers in exchange for diversion—"

"What's diversion?" Eric asked.

"No jail time for minor drug offenses. They get diverted to drug rehab."

He absorbed this and said, "Keep reading."

"C.I.s were arrested at 6560 Austen Avenue." I looked up. "Where is that?"

"Somewhere south of Highway Fifty."

I tried to visualize the stretch of road. I remembered some empty fields, a rock and garden store, tile outlets, and auto repair shops. It wasn't an area I knew well.

There were no parking places in front of the daycare center, either, so again Eric had to circle the block while I went in to get Rebecca. After Rebecca and I were back in the car, with Rebecca strapped into her car seat in the back, Eric pulled back into traffic. "Go on," he said.

"The C.I's were stopped by the police on January eleventh. They spent two days negotiating with the prosecutor, then agreed to cooperate in exchange for leniency. They showed a phone message they had received earlier at six fifteen p.m. from their supplier. C.I.'s were deemed reliable when one C.I. knocked on the door of the supplier's residence at thirty-four thirty-nine River Park Drive, and emerged moments later with a jacket containing a black shaving bag with a blue stripe which contained ten ounces of methamphetamine—"

"They did swipe one of my bags! Good thing we didn't ask for prints."

I closed the file and said, "I can't read this in the car. I'm getting dizzy. The handwriting is ridiculously bad."

The twins were back from school, in their rooms. "We have some more discovery," I called as we came into the house. "Defense team meeting in the dining room. I have copies for both of you."

The twins sat at the dining room table. I handed them each a copy of the file. "What messy writing," said Nathan. "I can't read it!"

"I can," said Jocelyn. "It's not that hard. I can read Dad's writing, too."

Eric laughed. His handwriting *was* bad. Meanwhile, he booted up his computer, logged onto the Internet, and did a map search for 6560 Austen Avenue.

"I think we have our first break," Eric said. "Look at this map, Cassie. Isn't that near where Tom rented a warehouse?"

"I'll call Tammy," I said and took out my cell phone. She answered right away: "Hi, Cassie. What's up?"

"What's the address of Tom's warehouse on Austen?"

"Hold on a sec, let me check." She came back and said, "6560, unit D. Why?"

"We just hit a jackpot. Was his warehouse marked? Was

there any indication that his business was there?"

"Nope. No sign, nothing on the door. I don't even think he had a mail box there. He rented a box at the UPS Store. What jackpot?"

"Two confidential informants told the cops Eric was their meth supplier. Their motive for informing was that they cut a deal after being arrested for meth. They were arrested in the parking lot in front of 6560 Austen Avenue."

"Bingo is right," she said. "That links the confidential informant to Tom."

"It sure helps," I said. "Thanks."

I made some polite small talk, then hung up and went back to reading the police file. Much of the information was repetitive, different officers recounting their view of the same events.

"Look at this, Dad," Jocelyn said. "On this page, one of the C.I.s is referred to as 'she.'"

"Look at that!" Eric said. To me he said, "Do you think it was a mistake? Or do you think one of the C.I.s was a woman?"

"I have no idea," I said.

"Could it be Paula?" Eric asked. "Any of the women who worked for him? His wife?"

"Can't possibly be Paula," I said. "I think I have witness statements from all the women who worked for him. It could be a mistake. The handwriting writing isn't clear."

"It does look like 'she,'" Jocelyn said. "But I only see that in one place."

By nine fifteen I was worn to a frazzle. Rebecca finally fell asleep, and the twins were in their rooms, settling down for the night. We had to wake up early in the morning, take Rebecca to the day care center, and arrive on time for our hearing, scheduled to begin at eight o'clock.

A knock came at the door. Eric looked out the peep hole, and then turned to give me a look I couldn't read. He said, "Two guys are out there. One with sideburns and a long pony-tail, the other with a blond beard.

"Donnell Mayer and Jeff the Tree Guy are *here?*" Could it be? I couldn't have been more surprised if a genie had come out of a bottle.

Eric opened the door a crack and said. "Hello."

I went to look. There, unbelievably, stood Donnell Mayer with a yellow-bearded man who must have been Jeff, the tree service guy. Donnell stuck out his hand and said to Eric, "I'm Donnell Mayer." His voice was low and gravelly.

Eric shook his hand and considered both of them. "You must be Jeff," Eric said to the yellow-bearded man.

The man said, "Yup, nice to meet you," and shook hands with Eric.

Donnell handed Eric a folded up sheet of paper and said, "We need to talk to you because we don't know what to do about this."

Eric turned it over and found it was actually three sheets of paper, stapled together. Eric unfolded the papers, looked at them, and handed them to me. They consisted of a cover letter and a two-page witness declaration, all typed up, waiting for Donnell's signature. I looked again at the witness declaration and saw that he'd crossed something out and written in the margins.

I've already mentioned how big everyone connected with the construction industry seemed, but these two men were enormous, even bigger than Big Dan.

"Tom's lawyer gave me these papers," Donnell said. "She said she wanted me to give a witness statement. She asked some questions, but I didn't like what she was doing."

"What was she doing?" Eric asked.

"She put words in my mouth," he said.

"What do you mean?" Eric asked, keeping his voice quiet and flat.

"She wanted me to say something not true."

"Can I read this?" I asked, tapping the paper.

"Sure. Go ahead."

Paragraph six of the witness statement contained the following two sentences:

> *Eric Sanders, the homeowner, asked me if I wanted to buy methamphetamine from him and I said no. After that, he got angry.*

Someone, presumably Donnell, had drawn an "X" through paragraph six and had written something illegible in the margin.

Eric said, "This never happened."

"I know," Donnell said. "Tom kept telling me, 'Ask Eric if you can buy meth from him. That will make him really mad.' Another day he said he wanted me to ask Eric if I could buy his meth because he wanted to see how he'd react. Afterward he kept saying, 'Did you ask him?' I knew something weird was going on, but I lied and said I did because he still owed me two grand and I wanted him to pay me."

"You can't say something in court if it isn't true," I said, realizing as I said the words that I probably sounded as naive as I've ever sounded in my life.

"That's why we're here," said Donnell. "I can't sign it." He looked down at the table, then back at me. "She has me scared."

"Who?" Donnell didn't seem like the type who was easily scared.

"I'm trying to get my license. I've got some convictions.

She said she knew about my convictions."

"Did she make any threats?"

"No. She just said she knew about my convictions. She wouldn't let me tell her what had really happened. She just asked questions and made me answer yes or no. She backed me into answering her questions the way she wanted me to. She was very forceful."

"What made you decide to come here?" Eric asked. It was a good question. Admitting, in writing, that they had been associated with a general contractor who paid his crew with methamphetamine had to be risky.

"I'm sick of watching him cheat people," Donnell said.

Eric stood still for a moment, considering him. Then he said, "Come in," and opened the door wider.

They stepped inside the entryway. Both stood awkwardly, as though both hadn't spent months working in this very house. Donnell, in fact, had a key for a while.

"Please," I said, pointing to the living room, "sit down. Do you want some coffee? Or tea?"

Donnell shifted his weight from one foot to the other, like a shy teenager. "No, thanks, it's okay."

Neither of them moved toward the living room, so I tried the dining room instead. I sat in one of the chairs. Jeff sat in the extra chair we kept pushed back in the corner. Donnell sat at Nathan's place at the dining room table. They were stiff and uneasy.

Eric left the front door slightly ajar and remained standing.

I looked through the papers again. There was a cover sheet instructing Donnell to make any changes necessary for the purpose of accuracy. "So you crossed out the paragraph with the wrong information and you tried to write what really happened in the margins?"

"That's right," he said.

I tried again to read his writing in the margins, but couldn't make anything out.

Eric asked, "Did you say anything to the police?"

He looked alarmed. "No, never."

Eric looked at me, puzzled, and then back at Donnell. "Were you stopped by the police in January?" Eric asked.

"No," he said.

So Donnell Mayer wasn't one of the confidential informants. Eric looked at Jeff, who said, "Me, neither."

To Eric, I said, "Maybe we'd better tell them why we're asking. They might have some information."

"Someone framed me," Eric told them, "made it look like I was selling methamphetamine and got me arrested."

"It wasn't us," Donnell said. "Probably Tom."

"The police say it wasn't Tom. All we know is it was someone stopped by the police in January. Do you know anyone connected with Mullin Construction who was stopped for methamphetamine in January and made a deal with the prosecutor?"

Jeff and Donnell looked blankly and shook their heads.

I said, "You were working here at the end of December, about the time Tom stopped working at our house, right."

"I was working over at the Pinette's place," Donnell said.

"I only worked for Tom a few days," said Jeff, "in November. I worked on his house, and the Pinettes."

To help jog their memories about anything unusual, I said, "Tom stopped working here the very end of December. Can you think of anything out of the ordinary that happened the first few weeks of January?"

"I can't think of anything, except that was when he and his wife were going to split up."

I nodded. I knew about that, from Gina Snowden.

"Here's something that was odd," said Donnell, "after he and his wife got back together, he was sure he'd win the case against you. He was flying high."

Even if Donnell wasn't the witness against Eric in the criminal matter, we still had the hearing tomorrow to worry about. "I'll tell you what," I said to Donnell, pointing to the witness statement. "Why don't we do a more accurate statement? You talk, and I'll type exactly what you say."

"Can she do anything to me?" he asked. "She's a lawyer."

"What can she do to you?" I asked.

"I don't know. Maybe go to the license board and keep me from getting my license."

"Are you allowed to get a license if you have convictions?"

"Sure," said Donnell, "you have to put it down, then they decide."

I avoided looking at Eric. Later, I knew, he'd have plenty to say about how there probably wouldn't be many contractors if convicts couldn't get contractor's licenses—the sort of cynical comments I didn't like.

"Did you disclose your conviction on the application?" I asked.

"I put everything down, all the honest truth."

"Then I don't see how Paula Armstrong can hurt you if you haven't done anything wrong," I said, a comment right up there with *you can't say something in court that isn't true*, for wide-eyed innocence.

"I'll get the laptop," said Eric, "and the small printer." He went off down the hall.

"Tom owes me for the last three months I worked," Donnell said. "I kept telling him I'd sign it because I want to get paid. But I wasn't going to sign it."

Eric came back with the laptop and printer. When the computer was booted up and ready, I sat down to type. First I took down the basic information, his name, how long he worked for Tom, that sort of thing. "What's your address?" I asked, forgetting about the homelessness.

He looked alarmed at the question. Feeling foolish, I asked, "Is there an address I can use? Somewhere you can be reached if necessary?"

"You can use my address," Jeff said, and gave me his address.

Then we came to the meat of the matter. I said, "Tell me exactly what happened." I prompted him by saying, "Tom told you to ask Eric if you could buy meth from him. Tom said that would make Eric really mad—"

"That's right," he said. "He kept telling me to try it because he wanted to see how Eric would react. He said maybe he wouldn't give me my pay if I didn't do it. So next time he asked, I said, 'Yes I did,' because I wanted him to pay me what he owed me."

"Can I put here that you never had any conversation with Eric about meth?"

"Yes, put that down."

"Can I put something down about why you didn't sign Paula's declaration?"

"Okay," he said. "I didn't sign the declaration because it had things that weren't true. I tried to tell her, but she didn't listen. She just kept asking questions and putting words into my mouth. You can type that."

I typed the new paragraph and printed the new version so he could sign it. I asked him if I could keep a copy of the declaration Paula Armstrong had tried to get him to sign. He said yes, so Eric copied it on the scanner.

"Did you realize Tom was thinking about setting Eric up?" I said.

"Not at the time," said Donnell. "It just seemed like the usual way he joked."

"You can have a statement from me, too," Jeff said, "I can tell you a few things."

"Great," I said, and opened a new document. I started with his contact information, and then said, "Go ahead."

"You might like to know that in November he paid his workers with methamphetamine. He said he didn't have cash, so it was meth or nothing. Some people took nothing because they didn't want to get mixed up with that shit. That's when most of the crew quit."

I typed what he said and decided not to ask any more questions. I really didn't want to know, for example, whether Donnell and Jeff accepted meth as payment. I also didn't want to know whether any members of the Tom Mullin Victim's Club accepted meth as payment.

I typed the usual ending, that the undersigned swore under penalty of perjury that the above statement was true.

Jeff signed it and they both stood up. "We should go," Jeff said.

Eric and I walked them to the door. "I guess we'll see you at the hearing," I said to Donnell.

"Yup," Donnell said. "Tom's lawyer sent me a subpoena."

Eric closed the door behind them and turned the bolt. We went back into the living room and sat on the couch. While Jeff and Donnell had been in the dining room, I'd felt tense and careful, like a lion tamer hoping the lion would behave. I felt intense relief. We still didn't know who the confidential informants were, but we had Donnell's signed declaration. Paula was in for a little surprise.

Eric put his arms around me and sighed contentedly.

"Too bad it's too late to call someone," I said.

"Who do you want to call?"

"Everybody, starting with Eliza, then Gina Snowden, Bev Pinette, then Tammy Sherwood." I would begin each conversation with, "You'll never believe it, but—" The running theme ever since Tom Mullin took his first step onto our property was: "You'll never believe it, but—" The fact that Tom's witness came knocking at our door asking for help because Paula was pressuring him into lying was right up there with the best of the "You'll never believe it, but—" stories.

Eric squeezed my arm affectionately. About an hour ago," he said, "I was feeling like crap. But I feel a lot better now. You know why? Our doorbell rang and the guy we've been searching for showed up and gave a sworn declaration that I never tried to sell him drugs."

"You know," I said. "Paula is worse than Tom."

"I wouldn't say that. They're both pretty bad. He's a lying scum of a contractor, and she's a lying scum of a lawyer."

"I want to report her to the ethics committee," I said.

"I think you should."

That was the kind of thing that appealed to Eric, who felt that wrongdoers should get their just desserts. I was the one making the dramatic turnaround.

"Here's the problem," I explained. "Criminal defense types who turn people into the authorities are hypocrites."

"Why? If the ethics board investigates, she'll get a good defense lawyer."

"I just don't understand why she's doing it. She's a licensed member of the bar. She graduated from a respectable school. She has options."

"She's greedy and unethical," he said. "Why else?"
I didn't think it was that simple.

19

Melissa, Eric and I arrived at the same time, at 7:45 a.m., the exact time we were told to arrive. She must have left the Bay Area at the first light of dawn. Melissa waved, but Eric and I couldn't wave back because our arms were full. I carried our binder and the posters—Melissa had suggested that we blow up to poster size a few choice photographs of Tom's handiwork.

The glass doors to the building were locked. Inside was a security desk, but no security guard. According to the hours posted on the door, the building opened at eight o'clock. We sat on a low wall enclosing the courtyard with our posters, binder, molding, and plumbing contraption on the sidewalk in front of us.

Bill, the city inspector who said he'd testify for us, came walking down the street, whistling. His beard was closely trimmed and his hair hung over his ears. He wore a white button-down shirt, and jeans. "Hello, there," he said cheerfully. "How are you all this morning?"

"A little nervous," I said.

"Ah, these things are always a little tense." He looked at his watch. "I got to sleep in this morning. Usually I'm up with the roosters. No kidding, as in cockadoodle doo."

"Do you have roosters?" Melissa asked politely.

"Sure do."

"Really?" Melissa asked, "Where do you live?"

"The foothills. I like it there. The nearest traffic light is twenty miles away."

"Sounds nice," said Melissa. "I can see three traffic lights from my living room window."

Melissa and Bill continued chatting. I pretended to listen, but in my peripheral vision, I watched for Paula. I knew I'd recognize her even from a distance because of her distinctive stride. I watched each woman in a business suit, but none even remotely resembled Paula.

At eight o'clock the security guard opened the doors, so we gathered up our stuff and entered the building.

The security guard looked at the plumbing apparatus and said, "What the Sam Hill is that?"

"It's a piece of plumbing," Bill said. "Can't you tell?"

The security guard looked more closely.

"I'm a licensed city building inspector and I can vouch for the fact this metal thing is harmless—unless you try to run water through it."

I looked around. The security guard peering doubtfully at the plumbing apparatus would be the perfect moment for the arbitrator to enter through the door, but no one was in sight.

"It's our evidence," Eric explained.

"It looks like a prop for a horror movie," said the security guard.

"I rather think it would be more suitable in a comedy," said Bill.

"Here's my bar card," said Melissa. "It actually *is* our evidence."

The guard checked Melissa's bar card and Bill's city inspector identification, and then said, "All right," he said. "Take it in."

Through a side door was a corridor lined with conference rooms. Room number 102, reserved for us, was about ten feet square, and smelled dusty and institutional, with a whiteboard and metal conference table.

I would have to sit in here for a whole day, or maybe two, across the table from Paula Armstrong. The room had no windows. The table was so narrow that if people sitting across the table leaned forward and reached out their hands, their fingers would touch—not that I expected anyone to join hands across that table.

Melissa put the posters on the whiteboard ledge and the plumbing contraption on the far end of the conference table so it would be within the arbitrator's sight. We sat on the side of the table facing the door. Melissa indicated that Bill should sit closest to the head of the table, where the arbitrator would sit. She sat next to him. I sat next to Melissa, and Eric sat to my right.

At two minutes after the hour, a man who I assumed to be Mr. Day, the arbitrator, came in. He appeared to be in his late fifties with a full head of white hair and a face round and fleshy like a potato. He had a relaxed, easy smile and a serious demeanor. He shook each of our hands and we introduced ourselves.

"Ms. Armstrong and Mr. Mullin are not here yet?" he asked.

"We haven't seen them," said Melissa.

"Well then," he said. "I think I'll visit that coffee shop upstairs."

Just sitting at that table reminded me why I hadn't wanted to be a litigator. The stress was just too much, particularly in criminal matters or hearings like this one when you didn't know what to expect, when you didn't know which witnesses would actually show up, and you had no idea what people would say. For me, it was just too much adrenaline.

I stood up and said, "I think I'm going to find a restroom."

"I'll go with you," Melissa said.

In a corner of the lobby a woman in a business suit was talking on a cell phone. She was facing the wall. Her suit, more of a cobalt blue than a true navy, seemed too casual. She was average height and weight, with chin-length auburn hair. Unlike Jocelyn's Pulse Red, this auburn was more natural, the color more subtle.

In the restroom with the door closed behind us, Melissa asked, "Was that her?"

"Could be. Her hair used to be brown."

On our way back to the conference room, Melissa and I crossed the lobby again. The auburn-haired woman was still in a corner on a cell phone. In the conference room, the arbitrator was arranging his papers at the head of the table. He had our binder, and the manila envelope presumably containing Tom's evidence. It was now ten minutes past the hour. I sat down between Eric and Melissa.

The door opened. It was Paula—the auburn-haired woman from the lobby—her face flushed. Seeing her again after more than fourteen years was something of a shock. She had a sturdy, athletic build. The way she held herself with her shoulders back and her chin up gave her a powerful presence.

To the arbitrator, she said, "You must be Mr. Day." She extended her hand. "I'm Paula. I've just gotten a hold of my client. He's running a little late."

Eric and I looked at each other. Eric's expression was composed, but I saw the glee in his eyes. Why hadn't we figured Tom would be late? When had Tom ever been on time? With luck, he might not show up at all.

Paula said, "Nice to see you again, Cassie."

I gave Paula a nod, but didn't move to shake her hand. This may have been rude but I didn't care.

To Eric, Melissa, and Bill, she waved and said, "I'm Paula Armstrong."

If Paula was indeed a crook, you wouldn't know it by looking at her. She came across as competent, brusque, and very confident. Still, I didn't understand how anyone could use the adjective sweet to describe her—until she flashed a smile at the arbitrator.

I remembered that disarming smile well. I thought Paula's smile was too obviously trying to be sweet to actually qualify as sweet, but I could see how someone who didn't know her could be fooled.

Still smiling, Paula said, "I'll wait for my client in the lobby."

After the door closed behind her, Eric said, "She may be waiting a long time."

"Well," the arbitrator said, standing up. "I'll take a short break myself."

When he was gone, Melissa spoke firmly to me and Eric. "Now listen to me, both of you. I want you both to sit there and have no expression at all. I don't care what she says. I don't care what Tom says. You are not to make any faces, and no laughter."

Melissa was right, of course, and it was a good thing she was there to remind me. I imagined myself sticking out my tongue at Paula as I whipped out Donnell's signed declaration. Obviously, that would never do.

"All right," I said, composing my features. In the tone of a child giving a New Year's Resolution, I said, "No matter what they say, I won't gag."

"No gagging!" said Melissa.

Bill asked, "Am I allowed to gag?"

"Yes," Melissa said cheerfully. "A gagging expert witness is one thing. A gagging party to the litigation is another entirely."

At eight thirty the arbitrator came back into the conference room. He looked at his watch, and sat at his place at the head of the table. What more was there to do? How long could he idle at the snack bar or in the lobby?

At eight thirty-five, Paula came into the room again, her face even more flushed.

"He's here," she said. "He's going through security. He was detained by circumstances beyond his control."

Eric and I kept our faces neutral. Naturally he was detained by circumstances beyond his control. As far as Tom was concerned, all circumstances were beyond his control.

Tom came into the room. He looked around and said hello. He was smiling his bashful, 'I'm a nice guy' smile. He'd shaved his head since I'd last seen him, and he wore a brown satiny shirt that wasn't buttoned all the way up, and no tie. The shirt looked expensive, but the color and fabric were wrong for a day in court.

Paula patted his arm warmly as he sat down, a gesture often used by criminal defense attorneys to make their clients appear to the jury to be warm and likable.

"All right," said Mr. Day. "Let's get started. I see we have our first witness. It's clear to me, from the complaint and counter-complaint what the dispute is about. In the interests of time, both sides have agreed to skip opening statements, and both sides have agreed to let Mr. Hayes testify first so he can get back to work. So let's swear in our first witness."

Mr. Day asked Bill to raise his right hand and repeat the oath.

Melissa had so edited her list of questions for Bill that it took her less than fifteen minutes to march through his credentials and personal experiences with the job site. He explained the permit, and what happened with each of his inspections.

"It says here," Melissa pointed to the record of inspections on the permit, "that you inspected the job site in August. Did you inspect the hold-downs?"

"I tried to inspect the hold-downs, but I couldn't inspect them all."

"Why not?"

"Three were missing."

"Did you let Mr. Mullin know that three were missing?"

"Yes, I did. I wrote up an orange correction notice and handed it to him."

"Did you hand it to him personally?"

"Yes, I did."

"Is this a copy of the correction notice?"

"Yes, it is."

"Were you present when the walls in the addition were opened in January?"

"Yes, I was."

"What did you see?"

"I saw that two of the missing hold-downs were still missing. One had been installed, but it had been bent."

"Do you recognize this?" she asked, handing him a photograph.

"Yes I do."

"What is it?"

"That is a picture of the bent hold-down."

"Did you observe why it was bent?"

"Yes, I did. The foundation had been poured in the wrong place. The frame was hanging off the foundation by two and a half inches, so the only way to reach the hold-down to the frame was to bend it."

"What did you tell the homeowners?"

"I told them they needed to hire a structural engineer to make sure the building was structurally sound, and to design a solution if it was not."

The arbitrator reached for a copy of the plans and the photograph. He asked Bill to show him which hold-down had been bent, and where the missing ones should have been, and exactly how far the frame was from the foundation. They launched into a jargon-filled conversation of their own.

To Melissa, Mr. Day said, "You may continue."

She showed Bill photographs of the electrical wiring Eric had taken in October, while Tom was still on the job. He said, "Yes, that is exactly how the wiring looked in October when I inspected."

"What did you tell Mr. Mullin?"

"I told him that the wiring was a mess. I told him not to put up the sheetrock until the wiring passed inspection."

"You told him this personally."

"Yes, I did. I looked him in the eye, and I told him not to put up sheetrock until he fixed the problems with the wiring and installed the missing hold-downs and got all of his work approved."

Melissa showed him photographs of the wiring as it looked in January. "Do you recognize the wiring in this photograph?" she asked.

"Yes. That picture was taken the day we opened the walls, in January."

"Did the wiring look the same in January as it had in October?"

"Yes, it did. Exactly."

"So the errors you found in January had been present in October?"

"Yes."

"Did Mr. Mullin call for an inspection before putting up the sheetrock?"

"Yes, he called three times."

"Was the site inspected three times?"

"No. It was inspected twice. Once, nobody was on the site when I arrived."

"Did the site pass inspection?"

"No it did not."

"Did you tell Mr. Mullin personally that the site did not pass inspection?"

"No, I did not. Mr. Mullin was not there, so I told his workers."

"Did you trust his workers to tell Mr. Mullin that the site did not pass inspection?"

"No. All Mr. Mullin had to do was look at the permit, which was posted on the site, and he would have seen that nobody had signed off on the inspection. If there was ever any doubt about whether he was free to continue building, Mr. Mullin knows to call our office. We keep duplicate records of which inspections have been approved, and which corrections are required."

If I hadn't been feeling so nervous I would have been enjoying the exchange. I looked at Eric. From the slight crinkle around Eric's eyes, I knew that he was thoroughly enjoying this. It was, indeed, impossible to imagine how Tom and Paula would respond to this testimony.

Mr. Day spent a few minutes writing in his notebook. Then he asked Paula if she had any questions for the witness.

"Yes, I do," Paula said. "Let's talk about the inspection you did at the Sanders residence on January sixth. That was a final inspection, correct?"

"No, it was not a final inspection."

Bill obviously had experience testifying in court. Instead of offering an explanation, he sat and waited for a follow up question.

"It wasn't a final inspection?" Paula's voice was so filled with doubt that if I hadn't known for a fact that it that wasn't a final inspection, Paula's tone might have led me to wonder.

"No," said Bill. "It was not a final inspection."

"What was it, then?"

Cross examining a witness is extremely difficult, as I had learned in my trial practice class—the class, incidentally, that made me want to be an appellate lawyer instead of a trial lawyer. But listening to Paula cross-examining Bill, it was easy to hear the mistakes. Paula had just asked an open ended-question to a hostile witness.

Bill said, "It was a combination structural and electrical inspection."

"But those inspections had already been done," she said.

"No, they had not," he said patiently.

She showed him the printout showing that Tom had called for both the electrical and structural inspections several times.

"Calling for an inspection does not mean that the inspection was done and approved," Bill said.

"But there is nothing here to indicate that," she said, pointing to the printout. Her second mistake was making a factually incorrect statement to a knowledgeable witness.

"Yes, there is," said Bill.

Now she had no choice but to ask him where. In response, he showed her the note levying a fine on the contractor for continuing to call for inspections when the work was not complete or ready for inspection.

She said, "But Mr. Mullin could have thought the inspections had been done, correct?"

The question was improper because it called for Bill to make a guess as to Tom's thoughts, but Melissa didn't object, probably because the answer was clearly going to help us.

Bill said, "A contractor licensed to practice in this state could never make that mistake. A contractor licensed to practice in this state must demonstrate the ability to read a permit and understand a printout from a city inspections office."

Paula didn't pause, or indicate she was changing the subject when she said, "The list of corrections you made on January sixth was a punch list, correct?"

Bill didn't smile, but you could see the amusement in his face. "No, that was not a punch list."

"This isn't a punch list?" she asked again.

Bill said, "No. This list requires major structural and electrical corrections."

"Some of these things are minor," she said. "Can you read number eighteen?"

Bill read number eighteen: "Remove insulation blocking under floor venting."

Paula asked, "Would you say that is a major or minor correction?"

"Minor."

"Then this is a punch list," she said. She sounded impatient, as if why was it taking Bill so long to admit the obvious.

"No, it isn't."

"Why did you list minor corrections"—her voice was suddenly sharp—"if it wasn't a punch list?"

I looked at Melissa, whose expression was carefully blank. This was absurd, and could go on all day. Eric wrote a note to me on his pad: "I wonder how much Tom is paying for this. She hasn't done any homework at all!" The weird part was even when it was clear she was wrong, she wouldn't give up.

Bill said, "The list contains minor as well as major corrections because we were trying to give the homeowners a complete list of everything that needed to be done so that they could get the project finished."

"So it was a final inspection," she said.

"No," Bill said. "It was not."

The arbitrator said, "We can move on, I think." Very politely, to Paula, he said, "I understand the point you are trying to make."

It irritated me to hear Mr. Day talking so politely and respectfully to Paula, as if the point she was trying to make was anything other than absurd and stupid.

"October was six months ago," Paula said to Bill. "Are you absolutely sure you talked to Tom Mullin and not a member of his crew."

"I am absolutely certain."

"How can you be so certain?"

Melissa shifted slightly in her chair. Bill said, "I'm certain because never before in my thirty years in this profession have I seen a mess like Mr. Mullin's electrical wiring. Seeing that wiring, and talking to Mr. Mullin was a moment I am not likely to forget."

"No more questions," Paula said haughtily, as if she'd accomplished something positive for her client. It was all too strange. Surely she was smarter than this. I thought again that they must have something up their sleeves. As the Godfather said, never underestimate your enemies.

"Do you have any more questions?" Mr. Day asked Melissa.

"No, sir, I don't."

To Bill, Mr. Day said, "I guess that means you're excused. Thank you for coming this morning."

Melissa stood up and shook his hand.

After he left the room, Mr. Day said, "I think we should take a ten-minute break." Mr. Day was the first to leave the room, followed by me, Melissa, and Eric. Once Melissa, Eric, and I were around the corner, we huddled for a whispered discussion.

"I'll tell you one thing," said Melissa. "One of your theories is wrong. Paula is not in love with Tom."

"How do you know?" I asked.

"She treats him like a little brother or a child."

"Maybe that's the kind of romance they have," I said.

Melissa shook her head firmly. "What I think, is that they're related."

"What?" I said. "No!"

"Can't you see the resemblance in their features? They both have full lips. They both have big foreheads. I think she's his sister, or maybe a cousin. That's why she's doing this."

I thought the suggestion was preposterous. Gina Snowden knew Kelly's family. If Paula Armstrong were Tom's relative, a sister or a cousin, Gina would have gotten word of it. Besides, I didn't think they looked anything alike.

"He's blond," I said. "She has darker hair. He's reasonably attractive. She has a face like a horse."

Melissa gave me a sharp look. "She's very attractive, Cassie."

"Pul-*ease*." I pronounced the word the way Jocelyn did when she was being snide:

I looked at Eric to see if he wanted to contribute to the conversation. He was listening, one eyebrow cocked. Seeing his expression, I realized how hopelessly feminine our conversation was. Of course he wouldn't want to venture into a conversation about whether Tom and Paula were in love, and whether Paula was attractive.

To bring Eric into the conversation, I said, "That cross-examination couldn't have gone better."

"It was just strange to watch," said Eric. "We spent all those hours preparing, and she just talked off the top of her head. She didn't prepare at all."

"I was thinking that, too," said Melissa.

On our way back to the conference room, I saw Tom's wife, Kelly, in the lobby, talking to Tom and Paula. Whereas I did not agree with Melissa's assessment of Paula's attractiveness, and I didn't think Paula and Tom were related, I did have the feeling from seeing the three of them together that there was nothing romantic between Tom and Paula. The three were huddled together.

Kelly stood with her arms akimbo. Paula touched Tom's arm as if to comfort and reassure him. It was not the way a woman touches a lover. It was the way a doctor might touch a patient, or a coach might touch an injured athlete.

20

It was Eric's turn to testify. Melissa led him through the story of how he'd come to hire Tom—how Tom brought him to the job site at the Snowden's house, complete with a construction crew and showed him the work he'd done in the bathroom and breakfast nook. Then she handed Eric, Mr. Day, and Paula copies of the Snowden's witness statement.

"Do you recognize this?" she asked Eric.

"Yes, that's—" Eric began.

"I object to these witnesses," Paula said. "These statements should not be allowed."

"On what grounds?" Mr. Day asked politely.

"We are now engaged in litigation with them. They cannot be unbiased in this case."

Mr. Day looked at Melissa who said, "We intend to show Mr. Mullin's pattern and practice, and his reputation for dishonesty. Moreover, the Snowden's statement is necessary to demonstrate outright fraud."

Mr. Day said, "I will accept the witness statements and give them the weight I think they deserve."

To Eric, Melissa said, "Will you read this paragraph aloud?"

Eric read the Snowden's statement about how Tom did not have permission to be on their property in June, that he'd stopped coming to work in January, and that another contractor had fixed Tom's errors and completed his work, and that moreover, all the work had been finished in May. As he read, I watched Paula's face for some reaction. She appeared attentive and curious.

Melissa asked Eric, "When he took you onto the Snowden's property in June, what did you see?"

"I saw a full work crew and tools placed around as if work was going on."

"Was Tom there?"

"Yes, he was. He introduced me to his crew, and said they were finishing up a project including remodeling the bathroom and breakfast nook. He showed me the bathroom and said he had just finished the tiling."

"Will you read the third paragraph of the witness statement?"

The third paragraph contained the Snowden's statement that Tom had never done any work in the bathroom, and that the bathroom had been remodeled five years earlier, by a different contractor.

Again I watched Paula for a reaction. Again, she showed no reaction other than polite curiosity. Tom, next to her, was slightly hunched, listening. Next to her, he seemed insignificant. I had expected to find him irritating, but instead he seemed unworthy of notice. I wondered if he had chosen Paula as his lawyer because he admired her boldness. Paula so passionately stepped into her role as his advocate it was as if our dispute was with her. I didn't want to find anything to like about Paula, but—except for her utter lack of preparation—there were those who would probably want to hire a lawyer just like her: A hard-hitter, a lawyer willing to stretch the truth, a lawyer out to win no matter what.

Melissa stood up, walked to the end of the table. She pointed to the piece of plumbing. "Do you recognize this?"

"That is what Tom built when he relocated our water valve."

You could see Mr. Day was trying not to react—his face was composed, but he held perfectly still and studied the pipes with his brows knit in disbelief.

Paula looked at the plumbing apparatus with the same disinterested glance that she might have looked at a fly on the table. So far, she was the only person I had seen who had looked at that mess of plumbing without so much as raising an eyebrow.

Melissa opened the binder to a page she had marked and asked, "Can you tell us about these photographs?"

Eric said, "This one shows how the plumbing looked after the professional plumber took out Tom's pipes and redid the work."

"Do you recognize this?" She handed Eric a sheet of paper.

"That is the witness statement the plumber gave us."

"I object to the plumber's witness statement," said Paula.

"On what grounds?" Mr. Day asked.

Paula looked at the statement and said, "He told me something different, so this statement isn't credible."

Melissa and I looked at each other. I reached for my pad and was about to write, "Is she going to testify to his comments?" But a note wasn't necessary, because Melissa asked Paula, "Are you planning to take the stand as a witness?"

"No, of course not," said Paula startled.

"Then what the plumber may or may not have said to you has no place in this hearing—unless you want to swear yourself in as a witness, in which case I'd object to your version of what he told you on the grounds of hearsay. We're offering the plumber's declaration given under penalty of perjury."

"Are you going to testify," Mr. Day politely asked Paula, "about what the plumber told you?"

"Of course not," said Paula, still startled.

"Then go on," Mr. Day told Melissa.

Melissa asked Eric to read the plumber's statement aloud. She then asked Eric to identify the plumber's invoice.

As Melissa and Eric marched through the next set of questions, I watched Paula. If she was aware that I was watching her, she gave no indication. She was as calm as if she were listening to a grocery list being recited: Tom blew up the kitchen light, he left the homeowners without water, and we often found him asleep in the backyard. *We need rice, and milk, and cheerios.* The homeowners didn't have a stove for six weeks, and the contractor spent two weeks manufacturing molding by hand that could be bought at Master Molding for seventy-eight cents a foot. *Apples, flour, and cheese.*

Melissa asked, "Why did Mr. Mullin manufacture the molding by hand?"

"He told us that it wasn't available for purchase, so he'd have to make it by hand."

Melissa reached under the table and picked up a piece of the molding Tom had made. It was uneven and splintered, looking as if it had been carved with a child's camping knife. "Do you recognize this?"

"Certainly. That's a sample of Tom's molding."

"Can you identify this photograph?"

"That's a picture of the molding as it looked after he installed it around the window in the new bedroom."

Melissa reached down again and handed Eric a second piece of molding, smooth and even and professionally manufactured.

"And what is this?"

"That is a sample of the trim we bought at Master Molding."

"Why did you go to Master Molding?"

"After we saw the molding Tom had made, I wondered if trim matching what we had in the house was available."

"What made you think it might be?"

"Each contractor I interviewed looked at the molding in our house and told us it could be matched exactly. What Tom made was a mess, so I decided to go looking in stores."

Mr. Day reached for the samples of molding and peered closely at them. Tom seemed relaxed, leaning back in his chair, as if waiting patiently for his turn to tell the arbitrator the real truth. I considered the possibility that Tom genuinely believed his version. Just suppose he genuinely believed that the final inspection had been done on January sixth, that the list the inspectors made that day was a punch list, and therefore the remainder of the contract had been due? Just suppose he was truly insane.

Tom didn't appear worried or distressed at all. Was that an act? Or was he genuinely not worried? I was worried, and not just about the criminal matter. I was worried about this hearing, and we had piles and piles of evidence. I looked at Eric to do a comparison. You could see Eric's tension. Eric gave the impression of someone sitting in a court of law giving testimony that could affect him to the tune of $30,000 or more. Tom could have been watching a television show.

Tom rolled a pencil on the table. Paula put out her hand to stop him.

Melissa asked, "Did you ever drive past Tom's house?"

"Yes," Eric said, "once."

"Why?"

"We were deciding whether it would be worth trying to

get reimbursed for our losses. One of Cassie's books said we needed to find out if he had any assets. We figured he'd have equity, but we drove by his house to make sure there was really a house standing up. With Tom, you can't be sure, particularly if he did some of the construction himself."

Melissa gave Eric a look to tell him that such embellishments were not necessary. "How long were you in front of his house?" she asked.

"I thought maybe two or three minutes, long enough to look. But we watched that video and timed it, so we know we stopped there for thirty-five seconds."

"I have no further questions," Melissa said.

"Well then," said the arbitrator. "I think it's time for a lunch break. We'll meet back here in forty-five minutes."

The moment the three of us—me Eric and Melissa—were around the corner, Eric said, "Something is going on. The kids have been sending me text messages for the past hour."

I never saw him glance at his phone, but he must have. He clicked a few buttons, read his screen, brightened and said, "Holy shit!"

"What?" I demanded.

"Read this," he handed me his phone. Nathan had texted: "We got it. The call was made from the house at 6:15 on Jan. 13. We have proof Dad didn't do it."

I looked at Eric and tried to figure out what they came up with. January thirteenth? The date rang a bell. I remembered reading that the C.I.s had been stopped on January eleventh and reached a deal two days later. The C.I.s said the call was made from our house to the cell phone the evening they reached the deal. The call would have been made January thirteenth.

"Let me see a calendar," I said. Eric clicked another button and a calendar came up on his phone. January thirteenth was a Tuesday.

I snapped my fingers. "That's right! Nathan's lucky day, Tuesday, January thirteenth! That was the day he was grounded, the evening we went to back-to-school night. We were all at the school between six and seven o'clock."

"Let's go," Eric said.

Rebecca was at a drop-off daycare center over on "I" Street, ten blocks away. "You'll have to drop me off at the daycare. I need to nurse Rebecca."

"I'll stay here for lunch," said Melissa. "I don't want to slow you down."

"All right," Eric said. Then, to me, he said, "Come on. We don't have much time. I have to get home, find out what the kids have, and get back."

Exactly thirty minutes from the time Eric dropped me off at the daycare center, he returned. I was waiting by the curb. I got into the car and he said, "I got it all. Our kids are brilliant. They got copies of the sign-in sheets from back-to-school night from the school office. Look."

He handed me about a half dozen sheets stapled together. There was Eric's signature, showing that he visited each of Nathan's classrooms between 6:00 and 7:00 on January 13th.

"We need to give this to Howard," I said.

"No time right now. We'll have to call him during the next break."

We walked into the conference room and everyone, including Tom, was seated at the table. I looked at my cell phone for the time. We were two minutes before the hour.

Paula was saying, "If we do a final brief, I'd prefer that we turn it in right away. I have a trial starting next Wednesday in Solano County. The trial is estimated to last two to three weeks." The rules allowed for each party to turn in a brief summarizing their arguments and adding any necessary explanations.

Her tone was boastful, as if having a trial last two weeks made her special. Well, so what, I thought. Weren't trial attorneys supposed to have trials?

"We'll keep that in mind," the arbitrator said.

A knock came at the door. Paula went to open the door. Jeff Wilson and Donnell Mayer stood there holding their subpoenas. Paula excused herself and went out to talk to them. She came back and took her seat without saying anything.

The arbitrator asked, "Are we ready to begin?"

"I'm ready," Paula said. To Eric, she said, "What kind of work do you do?"

"I'm a product manager for a lawn and garden company."

Eric had transformed during the past hour. There was an upbeat lilt in his voice. Ordinarily Eric wasn't what you'd call an upbeat, lilting sort of guy. He was still ultra controlled and serious, and you had to listen for the lilt, but it was definitely there. His skin had a glow and his eyes were bright. Well, no wonder. In a manila folder in his brief case were a few sheets of paper proving he was innocent of the criminal charges against him.

From the way Paula Armstrong pulled back at Eric's answer, you could tell this wasn't what she expected. "Product manager for a lawn and garden company? What does your job involve?"

"I'm responsible for a line of products. I direct both the marketing and the manufacture of the product. Or rather, I manage the people who manage the manufacturing."

"Does your job require technical work?"

"I do a lot of number crunching."

I wondered where this was going. Then Paula asked, "In any of your jobs, did you do any electrical work?"

"Oh!" Eric smiled and looked at the arbitrator. Eric had that extra-bright look you get after you've figured something out

"Go ahead," said the arbitrator. "Tell us."

"I told Tom about a consulting job I took a few years ago," Eric said, "helping to reorganize the technical support division for a television station. I told Tom I'd had to learn something about electronics."

"So you have worked with electricity!" Paula said.

"No," Eric said. He was still smiling calmly. Melissa had told him he couldn't laugh or gag, but she hadn't said anything about smiling.

"Electronics," Eric explained, "as in computer interfaces. That's entirely different from the electrical wiring of the house."

"But wouldn't your knowledge of electricity lead you to think you could wire a house?"

"Not at all. Electronics is a branch of physics that deals with transistors and devices like those in a computer."

"But," Paula said, "if you learned about electronics, wouldn't wiring a house be something you could do?"

"No," said Eric. "Does having a law degree mean that you can fix an air conditioner?"

Paula tensed at the question. The arbitrator said, "We can move on. I understand the difference between electronics and electrical wiring."

With something of a jolt I realized we were hammering Paula and Tom. I would have realized this sooner if I hadn't been so nervous. If this were a football game, the score would be twenty-one to zero. If this were a basketball game, the score would be fifty to zero. But I knew to hold my glee. In criminal trials, the outlook always appears gloomiest for the accused after the prosecutor has finished presenting its case, but before the defense has had a chance to put on its case. The truth is, most of the time the outlook appears gloomy for the defendant after the defense has put on its case as well, but things never look quite as bad as during and immediately after the prosecutor's presentation.

Paula asked, "Did you ask Tom to install a media panel in your house."

"No," said Eric. "I did not." He looked puzzled again and glanced at me.

"But you do have a media panel in your house."

"A media panel?"

Then his face cleared and again he smiled. "Oh! Maybe I do. Is the empty metal box with the phone wires running through it a media panel?"

"When you saw the media panel, what did you say?"

"I told Tom to take it out. I said I don't want it. We're pressed for space, especially in the closet."

"You didn't tell him that you thought a media panel would be a good idea because you could then wire the new bedroom for a computer and media center?"

"No, I did not." And then: "The new room is for the baby."

"After you fired Tom, who did you hire to wire the panel?"

"We didn't fire Tom, and we didn't hire anyone to wire the panel."

"So you did it yourself?"

Eric laughed, breaking one of Melissa's rules. Eric said, "I did not touch the wiring. The panel has not been wired."

"There are no wires in there now?"

"It is completely empty, except for the telephone wire Tom put in there. The phone wiring Tom did was done wrong and had to be redone. I can show you the invoice."

Paula said, "There are no other wires in the media panel?" She was using her scornful voice, as if she knew full well that Eric was sitting there telling bald-faced lies.

"Would you like to see a picture," he asked, "taken Monday?"

Paula said, "That won't be necessary."

The arbitrator said, "I'd like to see it."

I flipped open the binder—I was the most familiar with the placement of the photographs—and pulled out the page with photos we'd taken of the closet. One showed inside the media panel. The arbitrator looked at the pictures. Paula and Tom both moved to look over his shoulder. The metal box was empty except for the telephone wire.

"What's the date of this picture?" Paula asked.

"Monday," Eric said. "Three days ago. I took the pictures with a digital camera, so I can show you the dates and times they were taken."

I handed the arbitrator the printout with photograph numbers and dates. He read the printout, and then wrote something in his notebook.

Tom was leaning back on two legs of his chair. Nathan had a habit of doing that. I was forever saying, 'Nathan, keep all four legs on the ground.' The reason for Nathan's placement at the dining room table was so if he ever did fall, there wouldn't be anything behind him.

Paula tapped Tom's chair. She said, "Sit right," exactly the way a mother might speak to a child. Tom obeyed with a timid grin.

Paula said, "Let's talk about the night you were without

water."

"Which night?" Eric asked. "We were without water two nights."

Paula sat up straighter. "We'll talk about both nights. Did you try to call Tom?"

"Yes, I did."

"What happened?"

"First I tried to call his cell phone. The recording told me that his voice mailbox was full, so I couldn't leave any messages—"

"So you never reached Tom on his phone?"

"I didn't finish answering your question about what happened when I tried to call him."

"You said that you couldn't leave a message."

"That's what happened when I tried to call his cell phone the first night. Would you like to know what happened when I tried to call his house phone?"

When confronted with Eric's question—admittedly not what an attorney conducting a cross examination was used to—Paula showed her annoyance. She obviously didn't know Eric had tried to call on the house phone. Now she was in a difficult spot. If she said no, she didn't want to know what happened when Eric called on the house phone, the arbitrator would wonder what had happened. If she said yes, she was opening herself up to testimony that she probably wouldn't want to hear.

The arbitrator asked Eric, "What happened when you called Tom's house phone?"

"When I couldn't leave a message on his cell phone, I did an Internet search for his home number. I found this listing." He opened one of the binders and took out a printout. "It's a number for T & K Mullin on McCauley Drive. At the time

I didn't know that they lived on McCauley Drive, but I knew his wife's name was Kelly, and I knew he lived in that general area."

Eric handed the printout to the arbitrator. The date on the printout—which I had highlighted with yellow—showed that phone number had been printed on December 22nd. Both Tom and Paula leaned over to look at the printout.

"Did you call the number?" asked the arbitrator.

"Yes," Eric said. "I did."

"What happened?" The arbitrator asked, obviously very interested.

"A woman answered. She said, 'Nobody named Tom Mullin lives here and hung up."

Paula held perfectly still. I suspected she was trying to think of a way to discredit Eric's testimony.

There was a sudden clattering. Tom's chair fell backward and he tumbled to the floor. Paula looked down at him, startled. "Tom!" Paula said, "Are you all right?"

"I'm fine," he said, standing up and brushing off his pant leg as if he had fallen into dirt. He wasn't trying to be comic—he seemed dazed, and brushing his pant leg was like an unconscious movement. He blinked, and then gave his head a shake. He put the chair back on its legs.

"Should we take a break?" Mr. Day asked.

"I'm all right," said Tom. "Really."

When Tom was back in his chair, Paula handed Eric a copy of the contract and asked a question about one of the paragraphs. Eric said, "I'm going to let my wife answer the questions about the contract."

"Yes, that's right." Suddenly Paula Armstrong's voice went sharp and piercing. "Your wife is the *lawyer*, isn't she."

She said the word 'lawyer' in a tone one might have said

'baby-killer' or 'axe-murderer.' Both Melissa and Mr. Day looked up. You couldn't ignore Paula's sudden change of tone. Tammy had told me that when Tom talked about me, he made me sound like a conniving lawyer taking advantage of a poor ignorant contractor. I suspected this explained Paula's sudden disdain, as if she herself wasn't also a lawyer. I wanted to reach across the table and slap her face.

Eric looked calmly at Paula and put his palms flat on the table. "Yes," he said. "My wife is a lawyer. She is the *honest* kind of lawyer who doesn't help people cheat."

Paula sat perfectly still. Then her face went red.

Mr. Day said, "Maybe we should take a break now."

Nobody moved. Eric sat firmly in his chair. I knew he was too stubborn to be the first to leave the room. Eric would feel that the first person to leave the room would appear to be running away. The arbitrator didn't move, either. Perhaps he was afraid of what might happen in his absence.

Melissa picked up the empty water pitcher and said, "I'll go get some water."

That seemed to give Paula the courage to make her getaway. She excused herself. Once she was gone, Eric and I, left, too. Eric and I waited in the corridor for Melissa to return the water pitcher, then went out the main entrance and turned down G Street.

Melissa told Eric, "She deserved it. But don't do it again, okay?"

"I'll try not to," Eric said, clearly pleased with himself. Then he laughed and said, "Wasn't it completely typical of Tom to fall out of his chair right on his ass?"

"Very symbolic," I said.

"Hey!" Eric said. "I have to make a phone call! What's Howard's number?"

I handed him my phone, which had Howard's number entered into my contacts.

While he called to tell Howard what we had, Melissa said to me, "I'll tell you something. I sat in the lobby while you were gone for lunch. I pretended to read my notes, but I could see the three of them. I kept thinking there was something odd about Kelly. She seemed to be in charge. She seemed to be directing Paula and giving them both instructions."

"I'd always figured she was just his patsy," I said.

I remembered someone at the Tom Mullin Victim's Club party saying she was as bad as he was. *She just wants to live in a fancy house*, someone else had said. Kelly and Tom had been on the verge of splitting up in January, but reconciled, and, according to Donnell Mayer, after reconciling, Tom had been smugly certain they'd win.

Eric hung up and handed me my phone. "Howard said to drop off the papers after the hearing. He'll be in the office until 6:00."

21

Melissa was staying at our house that night. We'd made up a bed for her in Rebecca's room, and put Rebecca's crib in our room. I gave Melissa directions back to the house and called the twins and told them to make her feel welcome. Meanwhile, Eric and I headed over to Howard's office.

The door to Howard's office was locked when we arrived. His office staff had probably left for the evening. We knocked and heard his footsteps inside. He opened the door and said, "Come in. Sit down."

We were seated in his conference room when he said, "What have you got?"

Eric showed Howard where the police report said the call from our house had been made at 6:15, and said, "That was the kids' back-to-school night. I was at the school from 6:00 to 7:00. These are copies of the sign-in sheets. Those are my signatures. The originals are at McIntosh Middle School."

Howard looked at the sign-in sheets and the dates in the police report. "This is excellent," he said.

"There's more," I said. "The two C.I.s were stopped by the police at 6560 Austen Avenue. That is the parking lot in front of Tom Mullin's warehouse. His warehouse isn't marked, but he was the tenant in unit D."

"I'll talk to the prosecutor tomorrow," Howard said. "He's not going to like it if he believes a confidential informant lied to him."

Back in the car, I turned on my cell phone. I had five messages. Bev Pinette, Gina Snowden, Tammy Sherwood, my parents, and Eliza called to find out how the hearing had gone. One by one, I called everyone back and said, "I can't talk. I need to go home and go to sleep. I'll call you tomorrow when the hearing is over."

Driving down our street calmed me. The canopy of branches was a barely-there, luminescent green. Pink buds were opening.

"What are you thinking?" Eric asked, as he pulled into the driveway.

"Paula needs to be stopped. What she's doing is too hurtful."

"I agree. A crooked contractor and an unethical lawyer make a strong partnership. He trashes the house. She files a lien and a lawsuit threatening to foreclose. Most people pay to get rid of the lawsuit. It's safe and bloodless. No need for a gun, and much more efficient than armed robbery. A robber only gets whatever cash is on hand. A lawyer can go for the equity in a house."

He pulled into the driveway. The moment we walked into the house, I shouted, "Jocelyn! Nathan! Where are my star detectives?"

The star detectives were in the living room with Melissa. Evidently they'd told her the whole story, and now it was our turn to hear it.

"I couldn't read a word of that messy handwriting," Nathan said. "Those police officers write worse than I did in third grade—"

"So I read it aloud," Jocelyn said, "one word at a time so we could think about it. I was reading how they were stopped by the police on January eleventh and made the call two days later. Nathan shouted 'My lucky day! January thirteenth!'"

"And what do you think Jocelyn said?" Nathan said. "She started arguing, telling me that the *un*lucky day was *Friday* the thirteenth, and I told her not in South America."

"We told the principal we really needed copies of the sign-in sheets," Jocelyn said. "We told her you'd explain later. So she said the secretary could make copies for us."

"You two are beyond awesome," I said.

Dinner was a casserole Eric had cooked the day before. Shortly before dinner, I fell asleep in the rocking chair holding Rebecca. I came awake briefly as Eric took Rebecca from my arms and put her in her crib. I slept through dinner. The next time I woke up was when Rebecca was hungry again at midnight. After Rebecca fell back asleep, I ate standing in front of the refrigerator. I fell asleep again just after one.

The next morning, Eric said, "Look what I found."

He showed me a printout from the Solano County Superior Court web page. "That trial she had scheduled for next week," he explained as I was reading, "was canceled ten days ago because the parties reached a settlement agreement."

"What a liar," I said.

He said, "She's just like him."

They were both liars, but I didn't think they were alike. Tom seemed to be playing a game. Paula seemed to be posturing, and fighting for her life.

22

Melissa, Eric and I were the first to arrive at the conference room. Eric put the printout from the Solano County Superior Court web page at Paula's place at the table. Mr. Day came in, smiled, and sat down.

Paula came in next. I watched her face as she read the printout. She seemed slightly amused, and not the least bit embarrassed. Lying and getting caught, to Paula Armstrong, appeared to have no significance. Maybe Eric was right. Maybe she was like Tom. Maybe like Tom, something was just wired wrong and the moral parts of her brain were missing. It seemed to me that if Paula had any moral sense, she'd have some anxiety about the fact that today Tom Mullin would testify under oath.

Mr. Day looked at his watch. It was four minutes after eight. To Paula, he said, "I assume your client is on his way."

"He is. I just talked to him. He'll be here any minute."

Tom was only sixteen minutes late. For Tom, this was something like a miracle. Paula must have given him a memorable reprimand about getting to the hearing on time.

Tom came in carrying a garbage bag full of something lightweight. He carried the bag in front of him, like a trick-or-treater. If the bag contained something he intended to present as evidence, Paula had not disclosed the evidence to us on Tuesday as the rules required.

Melissa passed me a note that said, "What do you think it is?"

"Don't worry," I wrote back. "Whatever it is had to go through security."

Tom put the bag on the floor and sat down. He seemed completely unaware of the fact that he was late. His reaction to being late was like Paula's reaction to being caught lying— no big deal.

Paula said, "Our only witnesses will be Tom Mullin and Kelly Anders."

I looked at Melissa who said, "Excuse me. Will Donnell Mayer be testifying?"

"No," said Paula. "He won't."

"Well, then," Melissa said, "we have one more witness statement to present. We'd need to present this statement as a rebuttal to the statement in your claim that Eric approached one of Tom's workers about methamphetamine."

Melissa took two copies of Donnell's witness statement from her brief case and handed one to Mr. Day and one to Paula.

Paula said, "I object to this witness statement."

"On what grounds," Mr. Day asked.

"He's not credible," said Paula.

"He's your witness!" Melissa said. "He's on your list!"

"He's not credible," Paula repeated.

"Why isn't he credible?" Mr. Day asked.

"Donnell Mayer is a convicted felon."

Melissa was so startled that she actually laughed, breaking her own rule. Instead of pointing out that Tom was also a convicted felon, she repeated, "But he's *your* witness. He's on your list." She gave her head a little shake and said, "Surely you knew he was a convicted felon when you subpoenaed him."

Paula reddened, but persisted. "I object to his testimony. He is a convicted felon."

Melissa paused for a moment, no doubt to take the sting out of her next question. In an unusually quiet voice, she said, "Are we to distrust the word of all convicted felons?"

I looked at Mr. Day. Unless Mr. Day had entirely failed to flip through my binder, he knew that Tom was a convicted felon because I had made sure, when indexing the evidence, that I had given prominence to Tom's felony fraud convictions.

"In the case of Donnell Mayer," said Paula, "yes, we are to distrust him."

Melissa looked at Mr. Day, and then back at Paula. Gently she said, "He was Mr. Mullin's employee. At Mr. Mullin's direction, he was frequently on my client's property. May we make assumptions from this about Mr. Mullin's judgment and the sort of people Mr. Mullin hired?"

Mr. Day said, "I will accept the witness statement and give it the weight I think it deserves."

"I don't see why they need his testimony," Paula said.

She was indeed fighting like a caged animal. Why was this so personal to her? Wasn't it enough that she was taking Tom's money and coming into this hearing essentially unprepared? What more did she want? Why was she bent on making sure Tom could essentially steal from us and defraud us?

"We need his testimony," Melissa explained quietly to Mr. Day, "because in Mr. Mullin's answer and counterclaim they accused my clients of soliciting one of Tom's workers about illegal drugs. The contract has a binding arbitration clause, which means that this is the only civil forum for my clients to clear their name and get a judgment stating the truth."

"I will accept the witness statement," Mr. Day repeated, "and give it the weight I think it deserves."

I wondered if Mr. Day had attended an arbitrator training class in which he was taught to say, "I will accept the evidence and give it the weight I think it deserves."

Melissa asked Eric to read the statement aloud. Because the accusation involved him, it made sense that he should get the honor. As Eric read about how Donnell had felt pressured by Paula to sign a statement that wasn't true, Paula gave her first real reaction. She tensed, and her mouth tightened. I thought she was genuinely angry. Mr. Day, however, remained neutral.

When Eric finished reading, Mr. Day made a note on his pad, put his copy of the witness statement into a folder, and turned to Paula and said, "Are you going to call your first witness?"

"Tom will testify first," Paula said.

The arbitrator swore him in. Tom swore to tell the truth. On the pad in front of him, Eric wrote in small enough lettering that only I could see, "Yeah, right."

Paula started by asking the usual preliminary questions: His name, his occupation, how he knew me and Eric. She asked her questions in a strangely cheerful voice, and he gave each answer, quickly, in the same lilting voice, as if she were singing the first part of the song, and he was singing the second, in perfect harmony.

She said, "Did the plaintiffs fire you from the job?"

"Yes, they did."

"What did they say?"

"They told me to pack my tools and leave the job site."

"And did you do that?"

"Yes, I did. I packed my tools and left the job site because they told me to leave."

"Would you have been willing to continue working on the project?"

"I sure would have."

"Did you do your best to get the project done on time?"

"I definitely did."

His answers were so rapid-fire and cheerful that the performance had the ring of a puppet show.

Paula said, "Did you look for molding to match the plaintiff's house?

"Yes, I did."

"Where did you look?"

"I looked in three places, including Master Molding."

Eric had testified that the sales clerk at Master Molding had told him that they'd had that particular trim in stock continuously for the entire eight years he'd worked there.

Paula asked, "What happened when you tried to finish the work in December?"

"I worked and worked," Tom said. I assumed Paula had told him not to use his favorite phrase, 'I worked my ass off,' and this was his substitute. "But nothing I ever did was good enough. Everything was wrong. First they told me the molding I made was fine. Then after I spent two weeks making it all by hand, they found it at a store and told me to buy that. They blamed me for things that weren't my fault at all."

Melissa shifted in her chair. Mr. Day was watching Tom but not writing anything in his notebook.

"What kinds of things weren't your fault?" Paula asked.

"The telephone wires for example. It was the stucco crew that stepped on the wires and trampled them. I told the stucco crew to fix everything, and I thought they did. I don't know who crossed those wires so they didn't have a stove, but wasn't me. I hired Sam Larsen, who told me he was a licensed contractor, to do the Sanders frame. I assumed he'd moved the water valve first."

This was what Tom had been saying for months—nothing was his fault, it was all the fault of his incompetent employees and subcontractors.

Paula said, "Tell us about the plumbing work you did."

Tom said, "They fired me before I could finish relocating the water valve. I didn't want to leave them without water so I had to put a few things together in a hurry. I had to use spare parts from my truck."

She said, "Was the plumbing you put together up to code?"

Tom said, "Not the part where I had to reduce the flow from two inches to one half inch."

"All right," Paula said. "Let's talk about the hold-downs. Were the hold-downs bent when you installed the sheetrock?"

"No, they were not. They were perfectly straight."

"Do you have a demonstration you want to do?"

"Yes, I do." Tom reached under the table opened the plastic garbage bag. From inside the bag, he took four Styrofoam blocks about the size of cinderblocks, and several pieces of balsa wood. He laid down the balsa wood, and then placed the Styrofoam blocks on top.

"Hold-downs are the things that hold the frame to the foundation," he said as if lecturing to a class. "Imagine that this wood is the foundation." He held up one of the pieces of balsa wood. "Now imagine that these blocks are the wall." He placed a block on the wood.

Mr. Day was just sort of staring. In that moment, I thought Tom was truly crazy, like scary crazy. Tom's voice droned on as he lectured about how the hold-downs secured the Styrofoam to the balsa wood. Hadn't either Tom or Paula read Mr. Day's resume? Mr. Day held a B.A. and M.A. in architecture from Stanford. He was a licensed general contractor in five states, and here was Tom Mullin, lecturing him about hold-downs using Styrofoam blocks and balsa wood.

Paula was watching Tom's performance with the same rapt and pleased attention that a parent might watch a toddler doing his first finger-painting. I was now convinced that Tom was, in fact, loony. I thought about the enormous sums of money that a general contractor has in his hands at any given time. The price of our job was just over $50,000. The price of the Snowden's job was $75,000. The price of the Pinette's job was $65,000. That came to almost $200,000. Most people would feel a little giddy after collecting anywhere near that amount.

After collecting a few large payments, he must have felt himself a high-riding general contractor, employing people and firing people. Maybe he just rode too high and lost control. In November, he had no crew. You can't build three projects without a crew, particularly if your wife is pressuring you to finish her house. Maybe he'd thought Eric and I should have been more understanding of the difficult situation he was in. Instead, we applied pressure. We had a baby coming. The stove didn't work. The telephone didn't work. Why didn't he have any workers at the house? He would have been getting the same pressure from the Pinettes and his wife. The money was gone by then. He needed to pay his lawyer—obviously, for him, a top priority. The hundred thousand he'd taken out of his house wasn't enough. He needed money, quickly. That was probably when he increased the amount of money he claimed the Snowdens owed him.

No doubt he had whined to Paula about how we had been mean to him, and wouldn't give him a chance to fix the problems. How mean of us. How unfair to poor, poor Tom.

Also, how annoying that we weren't doing what he expected—firing him, failing to document damages, and then giving him money to make him disappear.

Tom took more Styrofoam blocks from his bag. He stacked the blocks in a row two deep, two high, and four across. He was talking about how it wouldn't be possible to install hold-downs if they were already bent. Mr. Day had put his pencil down on the table.

"Mr. Mullin," Mr. Day said, "I don't think we need to go on with this."

"I want to explain why the hold-downs were not bent when I was fired from the job."

"I've installed a good many hold-downs during my career as a contractor," Mr. Day said. "I understand how they work and what they do."

Tom put his blocks and wood back into the bag. "Then you know they couldn't have been bent when I installed them."

Mr. Day didn't respond to this. He looked at his watch and said, "I think it's time for a brief morning break. Shall we return in fifteen minutes?"

He wasn't really expecting an answer, so nobody responded. Tom stood up and stretched, as if coming out of sleep.

23

Eric, Melissa, and I walked into the lobby to find a startling sight: Two uniformed police officers questioning Kelly, who stood near a wall, looking small and ashen-faced. The officers towered over her. I caught her expression just before she saw us. You could see at a glance from the quiver of her jaw and her slouched posture that she was about to collapse.

"Maybe we should wait in the room," Melissa said.

I agreed. We were too far away anyway to catch what they were saying. We returned to the room. Mr. Day was writing in his notebook.

When everyone assembled again, Mr. Day asked Paula if she had any additional evidence to present. She said no. So she wouldn't be calling any other witnesses after all, and she wasn't going to show the video of us stopping by Tom's house that night.

The arbitrator looked at Melissa and said, "Do you have any questions for Mr. Mullin?"

"I do have a question for Mr. Mullin." Melissa stood up and went to the other side of the table and picked up the plumbing contraption. She brought it back to the end of the table where everyone was sitting and put it down in the center of the table, not far from Mr. Day.

"Mr. Mullin," she asked, "which part is not up to code?"

He stood up and pointed to the place where the two pipes came together and said, "There."

"That is the only part that is not up to code?" she asked.

"Yes."

"The rest is fine?"

"Yes," he said.

Melissa looked at the arbitrator and said, "May I have a short conference with my clients. It won't be more than a few minutes."

"Go right ahead."

Eric, Melissa, and I walked down to the end of the corridor. Melissa said, "I think we should end his testimony right here. But I wanted to check with you first. I think he's discredited himself enough."

"I agree," said Eric.

"I think so too," I said. What more did we need to do to show the arbitrator that Tom was either nuts or incompetent, or both?

So we went back into the room and sat down. Melissa said, "We have no further questions for Mr. Mullin."

Mr. Day looked at Paula, who said, "Tom was our last witness. We will not be calling Kelly."

Melissa recovered quickly and said, "May I have two more minutes outside to talk to my clients?"

"Certainly," said Mr. Day.

Once we were around a corner, Melissa asked, "What do you want to do?"

"I want to call Kelly as a witness," I said.

"What are you going to ask her?"

"I have an idea." I realized I was trembling. "I want to ask her about the criminal matter."

"But you don't know what she's going to say," Melissa said. "You have no idea whether she's going to come up with some outrageous lie, and if she is going to lie, you don't know how convincing it will be."

"If she does or says something outrageous," I said, "we can stop questioning her."

"But I don't know the facts in the criminal matter well enough to ask the questions."

"I do," I said.

Both Eric and Melissa looked at me. The entire reason Melissa was here, helping us was because I was afraid if I had to face Paula without an intermediary I'd end up screaming at her and wanting to strangle her.

"I can do it," I said.

"All right," said Melissa. "Just stop immediately if the answers aren't what you expect."

We went back inside and Melissa said, "Mr. Day, we need to call Kelly Anders as a witness."

"I object," Paula said.

We all looked at Paula and waited. Surely she wasn't going to tell us that she objected to Kelly because she was unreliable.

"On what grounds?" the arbitrator asked.

This time Paula didn't have a quick answer. She looked at Tom, as if to stall for time, and then said, "I don't see what purpose her testimony can serve."

Mr. Day waited for Melissa to respond. "My clients have a few questions for her. This is the only forum they will be allowed to present their evidence. This is their only day in court."

"We'll call Kelly Anders as a witness," Mr. Day said. "Can you ask her to come in, Ms. Armstrong?"

Paula left the room and came back a few minutes later with

Kelly. The arbitrator swore her in.

Melissa said, "My client will be asking a few questions. This hearing has taken an unexpected turn and I am not familiar enough with the facts concerning Ms. Anders."

Paula was becoming very predictable. "I object to the homeowners asking questions," she said.

Melissa said, "Informality broke down while your client was testifying. He gave narrative answers. He put on a demonstration with evidence he had not disclosed. The rules of arbitration allow for whatever level of formality the arbitrator feels is appropriate. If my client cannot ask a few questions, we will not have the chance to fully present our case."

"The homeowners may ask questions," Mr. Day said.

I leaned forward and cleared my throat. I'd been jotting questions on the pad in front of me.

Paula, startled, said, "*Cassie* is going to ask questions?" in the same tone she might have said, *The devil herself is going to ask questions?* Paula had evidently assumed the more controlled Eric would be asking the questions.

I ignored her and looked at Kelly. "Ms. Anders," I said, concentrating on keeping my voice even. "Were you stopped by the police on January eleventh at sixty-five sixty Austen Avenue?"

Kelly's hands were curled tightly into fists. "Yes, I was."

"Is it true that you were stopped for possessing methamphetamine."

She glared at me. "Yes."

Melissa gasped. Eric sat up straighter.

"Was it *your* meth?" I didn't need to know this, but I was curious. The rule of taking cross examination is that you're only supposed to ask questions if you already know the answer, but well, I wanted to know.

"No, it wasn't. It was Tom's! I was carrying his case! I didn't even know it was in there."

"Did you make a deal with the prosecution to get leniency?"

"Yes, I did," she said firmly.

"Did you lie and tell them that Eric was your supplier."

"Yes, I did."

"Did someone enter our house without permission and use our house phone to make a call saying something like 'I'll have the package ready between 6:00 and 6:30?"

"You don't have to keep asking all these questions. Yes, we set it up so Eric would look like a mule and we got him arrested. In exchange, I got off with diversion."

"Was someone else arrested with you?"

"Yes."

"Who?"

"You'll never find him. He cut his deal with the cops and went home to Mississippi."

She spoke as if Mississippi were a foreign country with no extradition treaties.

"He's gone to Mississippi," Kelly said, "and I have to take all the blame. I lied once and now they won't believe the truth, that the drugs weren't mine and I didn't even know they were in that case."

I actually felt sorry for Kelly. "Whose idea was it to frame Eric?" I asked her.

"It was Tom's idea. Now he's saying it was mine, but it wasn't."

Very gently, I asked, "Why did the cops stop you in the parking lot that day?"

"I'm not sure. Why?"

"You might have a Fourth Amendment defense if the cops had no business stopping and searching you."

"A fourth *what?*"

"Fourth Amendment. You have a constitutional right to be free from illegal search and seizure."

"Wait just a minute, Cassie," Eric said. "What are you doing? Helping Kelly with her legal defense?"

"I hate to see her busted for Tom's drugs," I said. "She was caught lying, so now the DA won't believe the truth."

Eric spread his hands helplessly and shrugged as if to say, 'That's my wife—helping the enemy with their defense.'

"Maybe we'd better get back to the subject," Mr. Day said.

I figured later I'd give Kelly Howard's phone number. If anyone could help her, Howard could.

"I have no further questions," I said.

To the arbitrator, Kelly said, "Can I leave now?"

"Do you have any questions for the witness?" he asked Paula.

"No questions," Paula said.

"You're excused, Ms. Anders. Thank you for testifying."

Kelly got up and left the room, slamming the door behind her like an angry child.

We all sat in silence for a few moments. Then Mr. Day said, "I think we can waive final arguments. Do you all agree?"

Paula nodded stiffly. Melissa said, "Certainly."

Mr. Day said, "I will have a decision for you within twenty days."

I watched Paula, hoping she'd look at me. When she did I narrowed my eyes at her. I hoped I was giving her one of Eric's *I'm going to nail your ass* looks.

That afternoon Howard called Eric to tell him that the prosecutor was dropping the charges against Eric.

Eric hung up and said, "Do you know where we're going

tonight?"

"Where?" I asked.

"We're bribing the twins to baby-sit and we're going dancing."

Dancing? We hadn't been dancing in years. Come to think of it, we'd never been dancing in Sacramento—always on vacation somewhere. "Dancing where?" I asked. The only places I knew in Sacramento were college hangouts.

"We'll figure it out," he said.

"All right," I said. Who was I to argue with a guy who just had the criminal charges against him dropped? But, *dancing?* Maybe you *can* be married to someone for sixteen years and not really know him.

24

Eric and I met back in graduate school on a bright day in July. Sunbathers crowded the grassy hills surrounding the University Rec pool, eyeing each other and showing off their tanned bodies. I'd been swimming laps and paused at the edge when, from the direction of Hutchinson Drive, came an upbeat rendition of "When the Saints Go Marching In." I removed my goggles and squinted into the bright sunlight. The university marching band in full uniform was marching toward the pool.

The band broke formation—men to the left, women to the right—marched through their respective locker rooms, and met up again inside the cyclone fencing. Some band members stood near the pool. Some marched into the pool using the steps at the shallow end. Others slid into waist-high water without missing a beat, holding up their instruments. There were French horns in the shallow water, and a few trumpets on the diving boards. Two marchers with crash cymbals hoisted themselves on the concrete island in the middle of the pool, like brightly-colored turtles climbing onto the rocks.

I pulled myself up so I was sitting on the edge of the pool, dangling my feet in the water. Eric sat next to me, his body small, but lean and muscular.

The band switched to the Jetsons theme song. Eric grunted and said, "What the heck?"

Other swimmers were exchanging amused glances, but this small and wiry man seemed downright annoyed. "This is funny," I told him.

"Don't mind him," said a man with a mustache sitting to his left. "Eric likes to complain. Yap, yap, yap." He gave Eric a good-natured punch on the arm.

To the Sound of Music's "So Long, Farewell," the band members marched to the edge of the pool and pulled themselves from the water. They marched back through the locker rooms toward the street, their uniforms dripping wet.

That was when Eric turned to me, stuck out his hand, and said, "I am Eric." Then he turned so that he was addressing his friend and me, and said, "I wasn't complaining. I was asking."

"I'm Cassie," I said. "I was laughing." His speed-o was distracting. I had trouble looking him in the eyes with his bulge showing down there.

With the band gone, others, including Eric's friend, resumed their laps. But Eric and I stayed where we were and exchanged the basic introductory information: I was working toward my teaching credential, he was studying for his master's in business administration.

That afternoon, I told Eliza about him. That was back when Eliza and I still relied on the telephone, before email and text-messaging took over.

"Well?" she asked. "Is he attractive?"

"I won't know until I see him dressed."

Much later, when we were planning our wedding, Eric, who took all things seriously, asked if we were stuck with "When the Saints Go Marching In," as our song.

"I don't think it will play well at a Jewish wedding," I said.

I didn't see much potential for the Jetsons theme song, either. And "So Long, Farewell," was out of the question.

We settled on the time-honored, *May I have this dance, for the rest of my life.* So maybe going dancing the night his criminal charges were dropped was fitting after all.

During the days following the hearing, something was bothering Jocelyn. She was going to school without a touch of makeup, a sure sign that she was on the outs again with Amanda and Kayla. Each day she came home from school and said, "Hi, Mom," her tone weary, then went into her room and closed the door. It wasn't like Jocelyn to shut herself up in her room. Ordinarily after she did her homework, she found her cat, Cocoa, and they snuggled up together on the couch to watch television.

One afternoon at about four, I knocked on her door. Jocelyn said, "Come, in," in the same weary voice. She was up in her loft bed. I climbed up a few rungs of the latter to look at her. Jocelyn was lying on her back, looking up at the ceiling, idly playing with the cord of her sweatshirt.

"What's the matter, sweetie?" I asked.

"Nothing."

"Something is the matter. Are Kayla and Amanda freezing you out again?"

Jocelyn raised an eyebrow. "How did you know?"

"Just a hunch. What happened?"

"They started picking on another girl, a seventh grader. They were laughing at how she writes her essays. I didn't like it."

"I don't either."

The next day, during third period, when I knew Jocelyn was

outside for P.E. and when Ellen Tyler, Jocelyn's savvy and observant English teacher had her prep period, I put Rebecca into her car seat and drove over to the middle school. "I don't have an appointment," I told the receptionist, carrying Rebecca in her carrier. "But I'd like to know if Ellen Tyler has a minute to talk with me."

The receptionist picked up a telephone. A few students walked by, but otherwise, the corridors were quiet. The students who walked by appeared solemn. There was something so serious and self-conscious about middle school children.

"She says go on back to her classroom," said the receptionist.

Ellen's classroom was down the main corridor, and to the left, clustered with the other English classrooms. She was inside, hanging essays on the bulletin board. "Come on in," she said, setting down a box of thumbtacks.

"Thanks," I said. "I just wanted to find out what's happening with Jocelyn and the other girls. She doesn't tell me much."

"Jocelyn is very reserved," Ellen said.

"It seems to me that Jocelyn is banished from Amanda and Kayla's group."

"Yes," Ellen said. "Amanda and Kayla have been making fun of another girl, who probably shouldn't be in the advanced English class, but I wanted to let her have a try. Jocelyn refused to join in, so they banished her. She eats lunch now by herself every day."

Nathan had a different lunch period. Not that it would necessarily help if they had the same lunch period. Nathan's friends were a large and boisterous group of boys who found humor in things like putting jumbo-sized paper clips in their ears. Jocelyn just didn't have much in common with them.

"I knew something had happened," I said

"Kayla and Amanda have an attitude problem, and every

few weeks, they pick on a different girl."

"Usually it's Jocelyn," I said.

"Often it's Jocelyn. There are others in the rotation."

"Jocelyn seemed to think they're freezing her out now because she wouldn't be mean to that other girl."

"That's exactly what happened. I've been teaching middle school for ten years. An eternity. These girls can all be mean, every one of them—except Jocelyn. Some may not realize they're being mean, but the way they talk, the way they form cliques, the way they judge each other is cruel. Jocelyn is different. In my ten years of teaching, I'd say Jocelyn is the only girl I've known who sees it all for what it is, and will not, under any circumstances, join in."

I had heard good things about the twins over the years. Nathan was sunny and likeable, Jocelyn, who took school seriously, was frequently the teacher's favorite. But this was something else. "Thank you," I said.

Before the twins were born, I had been warned that newborns are not cute. I heard this from my Lamaze teacher, my favorite aunt and uncle, and others. So I was prepared for my babies to have squished faces, or misshapen heads, or ears curled over. To my surprise, from the moment the twins were born, they were gorgeous. I marveled at how two such ordinary-looking people as me and Eric had produced such beauties. Babies in magazines and television commercials paled in comparison.

Jocelyn and Nathan were in a gymnastics class when they were four. I honestly believed they were so much cuter than the other children in the class that I worried the other mothers would feel badly, so I made a point to go around and tell each mother how adorable her child was.

When Rebecca was born every bit as beautiful as the twins,

Eric came to suspect this was some internal trick experienced by all parents causing them to think their babies were positively gorgeous, but I knew otherwise. I truly believed that by some miracle, Eric and I happened to have extraordinarily gorgeous children.

Shortly after Rebecca was born, we went to visit a friend, who also had a newborn. After the visit, Eric said to me, "They probably think their baby is the cutest in the world."

"But after they saw Rebecca," I said earnestly, "they couldn't possibly think that." Eric gave me a look but didn't argue.

Then a friend told me about maternal narcissism, an honest-to-goodness psychiatric condition whereby mothers truly believe that their baby is the most beautiful ever born. My friend said, "It's probably part of the divine plan to help the species survive." I figured it also helped with identification. A mother always knows which one is her baby because it's easy to pick out the cutest in the bunch.

Now that the twins were thirteen, I had to let go of the idea that they were the next beauty contest winners. Instead, I alternated between being intensely proud of them and profoundly scared for them. Since they'd started middle school, what I felt was mostly fright.

But when Amanda Tyler told me that my thirteen-year-old daughter was never mean, I was right back to a feeling of maternal narcissism as intense as when they were newly born.

When Jocelyn came in from school, I sat with her in the kitchen as she ate her snack. I said, "Your teacher, Ms. Tyler, told me something impressive about you."

She looked at me and waited. Who doesn't like to hear that a teacher said something impressive?

"She told me that you are never, never mean to other kids."

Jocelyn usually thinks before she answers a question. As a teacher, I had learned to recognize students like Jocelyn and make sure they got as much chance to speak in the classroom as the quicker responders.

"Is it mean to be rude to someone after they're mean to me?"

"Rude how?" I asked.

"Not wanting to talk to them, or just walking away."

"No, that's not mean," I said, but I understood that it was a fine line, like the line between justice and vengeance.

"I'm proud of you," I said. "And impressed."

I was also embarrassed. Surely Jocelyn had heard me on the phone, talking to Tammy and Gina and the others about how awful Paula was, and how Paula had to be stopped. I wondered how it all sounded to Jocelyn. Did it sound like I was championing the cause of the victims? Or did it sound like the kind of hurtful gossip Jocelyn refused to participate in?

25

During the weeks we waited for the arbitrator's decision, I accepted another client, Laurel, a forty-nine-year-old woman who was out one night in Sacramento with her boyfriend, Craig, a married man. They had both been doing methamphetamine. Laurel fell asleep in the back of Craig's truck. Craig drove into the Air Force base, past a sign that said, "All personnel passing this point are subject to inspection." Laurel woke up while the security guards were inspecting the truck. About the time she fully regained consciousness, the guards found a vial with traces of methamphetamine. Laurel later told her probation officer that during the few minutes she and Craig had alone before being questioned by officers, Craig talked her into taking the blame and saying the meth was hers so that he wouldn't lose his job.

The prosecution argued that passing the sign meant Laurel consented to the search. Her trial attorney argued a sleeping person is not capable of giving consent. He also argued that the sign referred to "personnel," and Laurel, who didn't work on the premises, was not personnel.

"The reason there are all those lawyer jokes," Eric said when I told him about the case, "is because lawyers make arguments like those."

"The defense has to come up with something," I said.

I thought the "personnel" argument was weak, but it seemed to me the judge erred in finding that being in the truck on an Air Force base was implied consent. I thought the defense argument was a good one.

I was at the kitchen table at my laptop researching search and seizure law when Melissa called to say, "We got the judgment. I'm emailing you a copy."

"Well?"

"We're the prevailing party. The total award is more than twenty-seven thousand dollars. The arbitrator ordered Tom to remove the lien from your house. Congratulations."

I was thrilled—until I read the judgment.

The arbitrator said that our allegation that Tom committed fraud was unsubstantiated. What was worse, he awarded Tom more than a thousand dollars from the invoice Tammy had made for him, the invoice of numbers invented from thin air. The arbitrator gave him $300 for tree service work, $250 for that silly media panel, and $450 for the manufacture of trim. For some unexplained reason, the arbitrator said that $12,000, not $10,000 remained on the contract.

The total still came out to $27,235 because, whereas the arbitrator gave Tom things he shouldn't have given him, he gave us things we didn't expect and hadn't counted on, such as every single penny of our legal costs and investigation costs, including what I'd paid the private investigator to pull Tom's criminal records from Santa Cruz.

Giving Tom $250 for that silly media panel that we hadn't wanted and weren't using felt like burglary. $450 toward the manufacture of that mess of molding was an insult.

The phone rang. I could see from the phone number identification that it was Melissa, but I was too depressed to answer. I turned off my phone and laid down on the bed.

I was sleeping when Eric came home. "Are you okay? How come you're not answering the phone?"

I opened my eyes and said, "Sleeping people don't answer phones."

"Why are you sleeping? We got good news."

"No we didn't. We got the judgment."

"Melissa told me." He made a motion as if swinging a baseball bat, and said, "Home run! We got every penny we wanted!"

"No we didn't."

"Yes, we did."

"Okay, the dollar amount was what we wanted, but that isn't what matters."

"Cassie, what matters is the dollar amount. That's the *only* thing that matters."

"Look at this. The arbitrator said our claim that Tom committed fraud was unsubstantiated."

"That only means he thinks we didn't prove it. He didn't say Tom hadn't committed fraud. Who cares about that, anyway?"

"Look at these charges Tom got from his invoice."

"Cassie. We said we'd be happy with anything above $26,000. This is above $26,000. That means we're happy."

Life was so much easier for practical people like Eric. I turned over and put my face into the pillow.

"I don't care," I said, my voice muffled by the pillow. When I was in a funk like that, logic didn't work. Soon I'd have to make phone calls and tell everyone about the judgment, but I just wasn't ready yet.

I heard Eric calling someone on his cell phone. I figured he was calling Melissa. He walked into the hallway and said, "She's a little down." He listened for a few moments, then said, "She feels like we lost because of some of the charges he gave Tom from that invoice." He laughed and said, "I'd hate to think how she'd react if we really lost."

Eric hung up and came back into the room.

"Now Tom thinks he got away with fraud," I said

"Tom doesn't think he got away with anything. He has to pay us a pile of money, everything we lost. Plus, he's probably in huge trouble with the cops for setting me up."

Eric sat down on the bed and said, "Think about how Tom is going to feel reading this page." He held up page four of the judgment. That was the page where the arbitrator listed all of our claims in one column and how much Tom had to pay in the second column. In every instance, Tom had to pay our full claim.

Looking at the list, Eric said, "He had to pay $3,000 to cover Big Dan's handyman work. He had to pay every penny of the electrician's bill. He doesn't know he had to pay the cost of the private investigator because the arbitrator just lumped all of our legal costs together."

"At least we have something to save face with."

"When you win," Eric explained patiently, "you don't have to worry about saving face."

Tammy Sherwood called me the following evening. "Go look at the Superior Court web page under family court listings," she said.

I went to look. On the family law case index was a new case, Anders v. Mullin. Kelly was the petitioner, Tom the respondent. Kelly had filed for divorce.

I emailed Eric at work to tell him. He wrote back and said, "If there's a divorce, they'll sell the house and everyone will get paid." It was like the practical Eric to think of that first.

"If so," I wrote back, "we'd better hope our judgment gets recorded before his house sells."

"No worries. His house isn't even for sale yet," Eric responded. "I just checked the listings."

Tammy called again the next morning. "Have you heard?" she asked.

"Heard what?"

"I guess Gina hasn't called you yet," she said.

As if on cue, my phone beeped to tell me someone else was calling. Gina Snowden's number appeared. "That's her calling right now."

"I'll let her tell you," Tammy said. "Call me later. Bye."

I pressed the "talk" button to connect with Gina. "What's going on?" I asked.

"Tom went on a rampage. He was so mad over your judgment, he smashed a few windows. When he knew the police were coming for him, he drove to the preschool and started whining that now he won't be able to see his daughter anymore."

The only part I could actually visualize was the whining. "How do you know all of this?"

"My nephew goes to that preschool. My sister-in-law was there when Tom came screeching up in his car. The police came soon afterward."

"I guess he's coming apart," I said. "Where is he now?"

"He's on a mental health hold. They're keeping him for three days."

"'I need to go tell Eric," I said.

Eric was sitting at the dining room table, writing email on his laptop. After I told him the story, he closed the laptop and looked at me.

Quietly he said, "Tom went to his daughter's preschool?" If there was anything that might get under Eric's skin, it was a parent not able to see his child.

I thought Tom's breakdown was Paula's fault. If Paula had been reasonable and settled our case before running up his legal bills, Tom's debt would be much lower. If Paula had looked honestly at the evidence, and if she'd been truthful with Tom, he might have had realistic expectations and wouldn't be so shocked.

Paula had said she was not convincible, as if being not convincible was a virtue, but it wasn't. Not convincible was just another way of saying stubborn and obstinate. Who did she hurt with her stubbornness and obstinacy? As far as I could see, she hurt everyone, including Tom. Did she feel badly about what she'd put everyone through? Or could she walk away from the scene of a wreck without even knowing she had caused the accident?

Eric said, "I can't believe I actually feel sorry for him."

I was surprised that Eric didn't sound happy about seeing Tom come apart. So many times he'd said, "We're going to nail his ass," but when it actually happened, it just wasn't fun.

Bev Pinette emailed me an electronic copy of the deposition her lawyer had taken. Her attorney was asking the questions, and Paula was sitting next to Tom.

> *Question: What was the outcome of your litigation with the Sanders?*
>
> *Tom Mullin: It was fifty-fifty.*
>
> *Question: So you did not lose?*
>
> *Tom Mullin: No, I did not lose.*

Question: You were not found liable for any damages on the Sander's project?'

Tom Mullin: No. An expert from the license board testified at our hearing and he said that I wasn't responsible for any of the damages on the Sanders property.

Ms. Armstrong: I object to the question and answer. The question calls for a legal conclusion, and Mr. Mullin is not a legal professional.

Question: Do you understand what "liable" means?

Tom Mullin: Yes, I do.

Question: What does it mean?

Tom Mullin: It means that I am responsible.

Question: Did the arbitrator find that you were responsible for the damages on the Sanders' project?

Tom Mullin: The arbitrator found I was not responsible.

Paula Armstrong: Are you answering according to your understanding of what happened at the hearing?

Tom Mullin: Yes, I am.

Question: So the arbitrator said you'd done nothing wrong on the Sander's project, that you were not responsible for any of the errors.

Tom Mullin: Yes. The license board investigator said that, too.

Question: An expert from the license board testified at the hearing?

To say that reading the transcript sent me right up the wall would be an understatement. I was enraged. This was the source of all Tom's destructiveness. This was what Paula Armstrong had been doing since the beginning—sitting by and letting Tom lie. Until now, though, I didn't have solid proof. This was proof. Even if Tom was deluded enough to believe what he was saying—and it was hard to believe he was that deluded—Paula knew better, and she was allowing him to give flat-out false testimony.

I called Bev and said, "If you really want to discredit them and make sure you don't have to pay anything from that silly invoice, see if your lawyer can get your arbitrator to make a finding that Paula suborned perjury."

Bev liked the idea, so I emailed Bev the witness list from our hearing and a copy of the judgment. Bev called back the next day to say her attorney agreed that their case called for extreme measures.

I was in the grocery store with Rebecca when my phone rang. It was Melissa. "She called me," said Melissa. "She's furious."

"Who?"

"Paula. Who else? The Pinette's attorney filed a motion with their arbitrator for a finding that Paula suborned perjury. When she saw the motion and the evidence, she figured Bev got the idea from you."

"For someone who can't conduct a cross examination, she isn't completely stupid."

"She's not stupid at all. Not that it took much brains to figure out that you were behind it."

"What did she say?"

"She said the reason you hate her so much is because she's representing Tom Mullin, who she termed an 'unpopular client.'"

"Does she understand that I am writing criminal appeals? I know something about unpopular clients. Representing unpopular clients is not license to lie."

"She also said you've destroyed Tom and now you're going after her. She doesn't believe she's done anything wrong. She kept saying she was just being a zealous advocate."

Rebecca grabbed an avocado. I took the avocado away from her. "Maybe Paula needs to learn that over-zealous advocacy can destroy a client," I said,

Rebecca picked up a tomato and took a bite. "I'm in the grocery store with Rebecca. She just took a bite out of a tomato. I'll have to call you later."

Later that evening, Bev Pinette called. "The arbitrator made the finding," she said. "He found that Paula suborned perjury."

"Congratulations," I said. "That should help your case."

"Paula was riled up over that motion. She kept arguing that she hadn't suborned perjury because Tom's testimony reflected Tom's sincere understanding."

"Can you send me a copy of the finding?" I figured the ethics committee would have to take note of this.

Bev said, "Oh, one more thing. It looks like Tom's house will be going up for sale soon. There's a lot of work going on over there. Looks like they're fixing it up to sell."

"The race is on," I said. "We all need our judgments recorded before they sell the house."

"That won't be a problem. Who would want to buy that monstrosity of a house? It's overdone. It's gaudy. It's completely tasteless."

I didn't tell her that one of Eric's maxims was that there's a sucker for every piece of property.

26

I was at the kitchen table putting together the complaint against Paula that I planned to file with the state bar association when my cell phone rang. "Hello?

"Mrs. Sanders?"

"Yes."

"This is Mr. Reynolds from the middle school. I have your son in my office. He seems to be okay, but you should come over right away."

I tightened my grip on my cell phone. "What happened?"

"A boy kicked him in the back of the head. It was in the crowded hallway during passing period. There were several witnesses. Our conclusion is that it was an unprovoked attack."

My entire body went cold. "I'll be right there."

"He seems fine, maybe a little dazed, or we would have called an ambulance."

"I'm on my way," I said.

Now that I was working more hours, Rebecca spent her mornings in daycare, so I could grab my keys and walk right out the door.

Ten minutes later, I entered the vice principal's office to find the office empty. A secretary came in and said Nathan and the vice principal were in the nurse's office. She pointed the way.

The only two people in the nurse's office were Nathan and the nurse. "He seems to be okay," the nurse told me. "He's shaky and in shock. You'll have to take him to your doctor to make sure. But I think he'll be all right."

"How do you feel?" I asked Nathan, sitting down next to him.

"My head doesn't even hurt anymore," he said, touching the back of his head. "But look." He showed me that his hands were shaking. His hands seemed so small just then, small and pale, the hands of a much younger child.

"The principal asked me if I want to have the guy suspended," Nathan said, "or if I want to turn him over to the police."

The vice principal came in as Nathan was speaking. He said, "The young man will be suspended. There's no question about that. What I told Nathan is that it's up to his family whether to press charges."

Nathan said, "I told Mr. Reynolds that I don't want him to get into trouble. I want him to get help."

Just then, I made the connection. "Is this the boy who stole your key?"

Nathan nodded yes.

This must also be the kid who inspired Nathan to ask about my legislative reform group, the one who the kids said used drugs.

"That young man doesn't need help," the nurse said. "He needs jail time."

I was considering how to respond to this when, earnestly, Nathan said, "No. He's sick and he needs help."

How strange, to hear my own words repeated this way.

"Why did he attack you, Nathan?" I asked.

"He said he heard me talking about him. I wasn't talking about him. I tried to walk away, but he came after me."

"He wanted to fight," I said softly. "But you walked away." And while walking away, he got kicked in the back of the head.

"Yeah," said Nathan.

That was when I learned that teenagers do listen. You think they're not listening because they argue with everything you say and they roll their eyes and make exasperated sighs and tell you to stop lecturing. But really, they're listening—so you have to be careful what you tell them.

I had a son who said the boy who attacked him without provocation should be given help, and I had a daughter who was never mean. And here I was, after Paula with a vengeance. My children surpassed me.

"Will you be pressing charges?" the vice principal asked.

"No," I said firmly. "But please take a message to that boy from me. Tell him we are not pressing charges. But I am a lawyer, and if he comes anywhere near my son again, he and his parents will be paying for the rest of their lives."

The next day, I sat down in Howard's conference room across the table from him. "I'm glad you came by," Howard said. "I have a question for you, too. Did you refer Kelly to me?"

On my way out the courthouse the day of our hearing, I'd handed Kelly one of Howard's cards and said, "He's really good."

"Yes, I did," I said.

"It would be a conflict of interests for me to represent her, since I already represent Eric."

"There won't be a conflict because we don't want to press any charges against Tom or Kelly. We have our judgment against them, we're going to get paid, and we're happy with that. In fact, that's the reason I'm here, to tell you we don't want to press charges."

He didn't seem at all surprised, merely curious. "Why?'

Because I finally learned the lessons I've been teaching my children.

"Because of all the reasons you expect from a bleeding heart liberal. Tom is going to get what he deserves. He's losing his house, and all his victims will get paid. His wife—soon to be his ex-wife—was busted for his drugs, and now she's divorcing him."

"What about Kelly?" I had the sense Howard, a criminal defense attorney for thirty-five years, was amused by my explanation.

"She's paying dearly for her mistakes."

He sat back in his chair and looked at me.

"How does Eric feel about it?"

"After something our son did yesterday, he agrees. At this point, we both just want peace. Everything is fixed. The charges are dismissed. We've been reimbursed. There's nothing more to do." Well, with one exception.

"Fair enough," he said. "I'll tell Steve how you feel."

I assumed Steve was the prosecutor.

"However," I said, "I would like to complain to the State Bar ethics committee about Paula Armstrong, his civil attorney."

"On what grounds?"

I told him how she helped him lie, how she had to know she was helping him bring bogus lawsuits.

"Maybe she believes him," he said. "Maybe she believes that all those people were trying to rip him off."

"She can't possibly believe that."

"How do you know what she believes? How can you *prove* what she believes?"

I showed him the deposition in which she sat back and let

Tom lie, and the finding that she subordinated perjury.

"Notice that she's not technically lying. She has an out, a qualifying clause. She's saying that Tom's *understanding* was that the arbitrator found he was not at fault."

I remembered Nathan's ability to distinguish between planning to get on the roof and considering the possibility that he might plan to get on the roof.

"That's the way lawyers lie, I guess," I said.

"Some would consider the ability to lie without really lying to be a highly evolved form of art. You can report her to the ethics committee, but I'm not sure how far your complaint will get."

I sat back in my chair and folded my arms across my chest. "All I can say is, no wonder there are all those lawyer jokes."

The Pinettes got their judgment, a whopping award of $58,560. They scrambled to record their judgment lien against Tom's house before the house sold. A few days after they recorded their judgment, Bev Pinette called to say. "There's a sale pending sign on Tom's house."

That evening, Eric and I drove by to see for ourselves. Sure enough, the sign said "Sale Pending."

There was something satisfying in the idea of Tom's victims getting paid from the sale of the overdone mansion he'd built for himself with money gotten from his homeowner-victims.

The next morning, my cell phone rang. "Cassie. It's Tammy. I'm in shock."

"What happened?"

"Gina Snowden just told me that Tom went on another rampage. He took a sledgehammer and did thousands of dollars worth of damage to the house. He destroyed marble countertops in the kitchen, the stone fireplace, hardwood floors, and bathroom tile. He's back in the loony bin on a mental health hold. He said if he can't have his house, nobody else can."

It took four weeks for a hired crew to fix the damage and for the sale to close. The delay allowed each of his former employees time to record judgment liens against the house.

Then, finally, one morning, I received a call from the title company telling me they had a check for Eric Sanders and Cassie Eisen for $27,235. "Do you want to come get it?" the caller asked. "Or should we mail it to you?"

"We'll come get it," I said.

Eric and I went together. We arrived at the title company just before noon. In the title company's lobby, also picking up their checks, were two of Tom's former employees, Kristin, the out-of-work travel agent and Carrie, whose father was a contractor. Both were grinning.

"Isn't this great?" said Carrie, tapping a table with her envelope. "Tom's still at the funny farm, so we don't have to worry about him showing up and spoiling the party."

"We've been making jokes all day," Kristin explained, "about baskets. We figure if they really do weave baskets in those places, Tom's basket is a complete mess."

"And when his basket falls apart," Carrie said, "it won't be his fault."

The Sacramento Bar Association held a luncheon. A justice from the Third District Court of Appeal was scheduled to be the keynote speaker, so I paid my dues, signed up for the luncheon, and selected salmon with lemon couscous. Sacramento is not a large city. It occurred to me that I might see Paula Armstrong there.

I arrived early and recognized a number of people in the room. Some I'd met while trying to get a position on the panel, one lived around the corner, two worked in the public defender's office. I sat at a table with the other panel members.

Paula came in alone. I first saw her bent over the registration table, signing in. I watched her, hoping to catch her eye. I wanted to see how she would react to me. She never looked my direction. She took a place at a table near the corner with her back to me.

The speech, followed by a question and answer forum, lasted more than an hour. There were about sixty people in the room. I thought the crowd was too small for Paula not to have seen me at all.

During lunch I glanced occasionally in Paula's direction, but she never looked my way. Once I saw her in profile smiling at the woman sitting next to her. Melissa was right—she had an appealing demeanor—when she wasn't snapping like a dragon.

As the plates were being cleared away, I looked at Paula's table again. The place where she had been sitting was empty. She was walking toward the door, briskly. I knew from the purposeful way she was walking that she had seen me and was avoiding me.

I set down my napkin and followed her out the door. Outside in the corridor, I said, sharply, "Paula!"

She turned. I was standing about ten paces away.

"I just want to know why," I said. "Why did you do it?"

"Take one more step and I'll scream for the security guard."

"Oh, *pul*-ease," I said.

"One step and I'll call security and get you for assault and intimidation."

I actually laughed. "You're the one who destroyed him, Paula. You let him think he could get money from his bogus lawsuits. You let him think he could get away with his scams. Don't give me any baloney about how you were being a zealous advocate. You knew he was crazy. You knew he was cheating his customers. Why did you do it? I really want to know?"

"I was doing my job. That's all. You just hate me because I took my job seriously."

"What do you mean you were doing your job? You didn't prepare at all for that hearing. You walked in cold. How is that taking your job seriously?"

"I *did* prepare. I spent *hours* talking to my client, going over every single detail. I was entitled to believe him, Cassie. Here's what I think: You destroyed him to get back at him for not finishing the project on time. Now you're going after me for defending him. Can't you feel sorry for anyone?"

"I'm supposed to feel sorry for the crazed contractor who tried to cheat my family out of thousands of dollars, and the greedy lawyer who tried to help him cheat me?"

"*Greedy?*" That seemed to stop her. "Me? Do you realize how much money I lost on all these cases?"

"What about all that money he was paying you?"

There was silence. Then: "What money?"

"His employees said Tom always paid you first. People saw the checks he gave you. One was for five thousand dollars."

She blinked and then said, "That was for work I did three years ago, and to repay a personal loan. I took all these cases, including yours, on contingency."

Contingency? She could see from my expression that I didn't believe her. Contingency meant that she paid all costs up front, and that her only payment would be a percentage of whatever she collected on Tom's behalf.

Still, I didn't believe her. "Why would you take cases like these on contingency?"

"You'll never understand. You're so damned uppity and you think you're so good. He was my client and I was trying to do a good job for him. And I needed the money. I wish I had done more to help him."

It still just wasn't making sense. "Are you related to him?"

"*What*? No." And then: "You still don't get it, Cassie. Since you're so good at driving by houses, why don't you drive by mine? Then maybe you'll be satisfied."

She whirled away, the flap of her blazer swished like the flick of a mouse's tail as she disappeared around the corner.

Because I was curious—and because I'd been expressly invited to do so—I drove by Paula's house. In front was a "foreclosure sale" sign. The house was obviously uninhabited.

If indeed Paula had done all this work on contingency, and a foreclosure sign in front of her house confirmed that she probably had, I figured that from our case and the Pinette's case alone, Paula had spent more than six thousand dollars in litigation costs. No wonder she complained about the high costs of filing claims in arbitration—she'd been paying the money herself. Meanwhile she had her office overhead and filing fees for the other cases. Plus, she was doing all of this with no income.

This solved the mystery of how Tom had paid for her services. He hadn't.

Suddenly it wasn't clear who had taken advantage of whom.

It also explained why Tom hadn't wanted to settle. People settled to avoid litigation costs. If he wasn't paying litigation costs, what did he have to lose by going forward?

At some point Paula must have understood she was on a sinking ship. Instead of looking for a lifeboat or asking for a lifeline, she'd become completely ruthless. It seemed to me that my civil procedure professor had been right: lawyers and clients, like marriage partners, come together for a reason.

I went home and threw the complaint I had prepared against Paula into the trash. *You still don't get it*, Paula had said. She was right. It had taken me a long time. I was much slower than my children, and more inclined to be mean.

When Eric came home that evening, I said, "I saw Paula today. Her house is for sale. A bank foreclosure."

He just looked at me. I was glad he didn't say, *Good, she deserved to lose her house after suing to foreclose on ours.*

Finally he asked, "Why?"

"She took our case on contingency—and the Snowdens and Pinettes, too. She had to pay all Tom's costs upfront. It looks like she lost everything, including her house."

"But why did she represent him?"

"She needed the money. Can you believe that's all it was? She wasn't in love with him. She wasn't related to him. She wasn't fighting for a higher ideal. She hadn't consciously entered a criminal partnership. She took his case because she needed the work. And she lost everything."

It was late summer. Eric and I were in the backyard on lounge chairs sitting close enough for our arms to touch. Rebecca was in her jumper. I had planted sweet peas on the back fence, and petunias in the place by the garage that got full sun. One year ago, I was seven months pregnant, feeling as clumsy as a walrus, and experiencing every ailment known to the over-the-counter industry. One year ago, Eric was already worried about Tom, but I'd still been optimistic. You'd never know, looking at the house now, that we'd had a crazed contractor.

"Do you know what we could use?" Eric asked. "We could

use a second shower. There's enough space in the laundry room to expand the little bathroom and add a shower."

"Are you joking?"

He looked startled. "No. Why?"

"You're suggesting that we start another remodeling project?"

"We know how to do it now. We won't make the same mistakes again."

I thought about workers trampling through the house again, and the noise of hammering and drilling, and the smell of sawdust and sheetrock.

"I'm not ready yet," I said.

But I thought that if we added a second shower in the little bathroom, I wanted the tile to be peach. Peach is such a classic color, so warm and soft. Also lovely in the little bathroom would be wainscoting painted white.

ALSO BY TERI KANEFIELD

A young artist badly in need of money bluffs her way through an interview into a job she is not prepared for.

To succeed, she must make room in her life for two people: Curtis, a deaf architect who has sworn he will never date a hearing woman, and thirteen-year-old Alex, profoundly deaf, rebellious, bold, and frightened.

With sign language—nimble and evocative—at its center, *Turn On the Light So I Can Hear* is about reaching across distances, the transformative powers of art, and finding a place to belong.

ABOUT THE AUTHOR

Teri writes novels, short stories, essays, stories for children, nonfiction for both children and adults, and lots of legal briefs.

Her recent books include *The Girl from the Tar Paper School*, winner of the 2015 Jane Addams Book Award and the Carter G. Woodson Book Award. Her first novel, *Rivka's Way*, was a Sydney Taylor Awards Notable Book.

Her stories have appeared in publications as diverse as *Education Week*, *Scope Magazine*, *The Iowa Review*, *The American Literary Review*, and *Cricket Magazine*.

Teri lives in California near the beach.

For more information about Teri and her other books please visit her website at www.terikanefield.com.

www.ingramcontent.com/pod-product-compliance
Lightning Source LLC
Chambersburg PA
CBHW070731280626
47159CB00023B/3071